SO-AFD-454

PROTOCOL FOR A KIDNAPPING

Books by Oliver Bleeck

THE BRASS GO-BETWEEN

PROTOCOL FOR A KIDNAPPING

Protocol for a Kidnapping

By OLIVER BLEECK

William Morrow & Company, Inc.

NEW YORK   *1971*

Copyright © 1971 by William Morrow and Company, Inc.
All rights reserved. No part of this book may be repro-
duced or utilized in any form or by any means, electronic
or mechanical, including photocopying, recording or by
any information storage and retrieval system, without permission in writing from the Publisher. Inquiries should be
addressed to William Morrow and Company, Inc., 105
Madison Ave., New York, N.Y. 10016. Printed in the
United States of America by American Book-Stratford
Press, New York, N.Y. Library of Congress Catalog Card
Number 75-133288

PROTOCOL FOR A KIDNAPPING

CHAPTER 1

It was snowing in Washington and I was thirty minutes late when the cab let me out at the Twenty-first Street entrance of the seven-story atrocity of glass and what seems to be dried mud that shelters the U.S. Department of State from the elements, if not from Congress.

I had taken Eastern's nine o'clock shuttle from LaGuardia and despite the snow it had arrived only three-quarters of an hour late, which wasn't bad, but the taxis had disappeared and it took another half hour to get one and the Washington motorists were, as always, astonished that it should snow so far south, but if you mentioned that Washington was about as far north as Denver, nobody believed you.

So I counted eleven wrecks on the way in from National Airport and remembered that when I'd last been there the thermometer had threatened to break all heat records for August. As I understand it, the nation's capital is allotted two days of spring and three days of fall. After that it's either winter or summer.

A Negro guard at the desk just inside the brown marble entrance wanted to know who I was and where I was going and who I wanted to see. If he had asked why, I would have turned around and gone back to New York. But he didn't and a woman receptionist signed in my name beneath somebody called Emanuel Cory and I rode the elevator up to the third floor and got lost only twice before I found Room 3931. Some of the doors along the corridor had valentines pasted or Scotch-taped all over them and I found the sentiment oddly reassuring. Room 3931 had nothing on its door, not even a name, so I walked in without knocking. The door didn't seem to deserve it.

The ash blonde sat behind a secretarial desk which was bare except for a blotter, a telephone, a calendar, and her folded hands. There was an electric typewriter behind her, but it was covered. She was around thirty and wore big, wire-framed tinted glasses, not much makeup, a gray tweed dress, and the patient expression of a person who has spent a lot of time waiting.

"Philip St. Ives," she said, making it a remark rather than a question.

"Yes."

"Won't you please sit down." She indicated one of the two chairs in the room. I sat down and glanced around as she picked up the phone and dialed a single number. There were the two chairs, a green carpet, and a framed picture of the flag blowing in the breeze. I didn't find it as reassuring as the valentines.

"Mr. St. Ives is here," she said into the phone, listened a moment, hung up, and turned toward me. "Right through that door," she said with a small gesture.

"Had I but known what lay behind it," I murmured.

"Yes," she said, smiled brightly, folded her hands, and placed them back on the desk blotter. I assumed that she was through for the day.

The office that I entered had only a single window that offered a view of C Street and the snow and not much else. The man behind the desk wore the brooding face of one of those small, compact loners who stand by themselves at the far end of the bar on Saturday night, nursing their boiler-makers and counting up their injustices. When the boiler-makers and the injustices reach the proper ratio, there's usually a quick turn, a black glower, and a roundhouse right that's thrown at whoever's handy.

He didn't rise when I came in. He just sat there behind his green metal desk looking as if the delicatessen once again had sent pastrami when he'd ordered corned beef. There was a phone in the room, two chairs in front of the desk, a carpet, and another picture of the flap rippling in the breeze. I didn't bother to look for any valentines.

"You're late," he said.

"I'm always late."

"Sit down. Anybody tell you about me?"

I sat down and took out a cigarette. He frowned at that and said, "I don't smoke," but reached into a drawer and brought out a round black ceramic ashtray which had U.S. Department of State printed on it in white letters.

"I also drink," I said.

He nodded, a little glumly, I thought. "I know what you do," he said. "I know how you live. I even know how much money you made last year. You made more than I did, but I'm beginning to believe that so did everybody else. My name's Coors and no, I'm not related to the beer people."

"What beer?"

"Coors beer. They make it out West."

"Nobody told me about you," I said, finally getting around to his first question.

"Hamilton Coors," he said, "if you want to make a note of it."

"I think I can remember it all."

"You didn't know him really well, did you?" Coors said.

"Who?"

"The ambassador. Killingsworth. Amfred Killingsworth."

"Not well."

"You worked for him."

"A long time ago."

"Thirteen years," Coors said. "Killingsworth hired you in Chicago. It was your first job. First newspaper job anyway."

"And fired me a year later."

"Why?"

I shrugged. "Incompetency, let's say. Slipshod work. No nose for news. Things like that."

"I've heard you were pretty good."

"Killingsworth didn't think so."

"What'd you think of him?"

"Professionally?"

"Any way you care to tell it."

"He was a better promoter than he was managing editor. He didn't like to offend anyone—at least not anyone important—so he didn't and the paper got a little bland. Even dull. He married the old man's daughter and after a while the only thing to do was to make him associate publisher and then publisher when the old man died. I suppose you had to make him an ambassador because of services rendered and money contributed, but I still think it was a sorry trick to play on—"

The phone rang, interrupting me, and Coors picked it up. When he learned who was on the line he stiffened into a kind of seated attention and used his lids to half hood his large gray-blue eyes. It gave him something of a secretive look which he may have felt would keep me from eavesdropping. The eyes were the only thing large about him. The rest was spare and small-boned. Even his face didn't have enough flesh for middle-aged sag and Coors must have been close to fifty. His chin formed a blunt, bony point, a wide, bloodless slash served for a mouth, and the base of his nose started close to his lip and then flared up and out so that you got a good view of his nostrils. His hair was the color of a cigar's ash, a cheap cigar, and it was thinning a little and he brushed it straight down so that it formed raggedy bangs across a high, pale forehead. His tweed suit was good, I noticed, but nothing spectacular, although he might have gone as high as fifteen dollars for his tie.

Coors said, "Yes, sir," into the phone, so I assumed that he was talking to at least an Under Secretary of State. He didn't much look as if he would say "Yes, sir" to anything less.

"He's here now," Coors said. "Yes, sir . . . I understand." Then there was an audible click and Coors hung up. He turned back to me, unhooded his eyes so that I could hear again, and unnecessarily explained, "That was about you."

"What about me?"

"Some had grave reservations. So did I."

"I still do," I said.

"We might yet use our own people," Coors said.

"No. If you could, I wouldn't be sitting here and you'd be back in your real office, the one with your name by the door. Seventh floor?"

"Sixth," Coors said and then began a close inspection of

the fingernails on his left hand. They looked to be nicely bitten. "So you're none too eager?"

"You know I'm not."

"It's all really quite simple."

"No, it isn't," I said. "If it were simple, there wouldn't be any question about using your own people. Or even the CIA. Kidnapping American ambassadors still isn't as popular a pastime as hijacking planes to Cuba, but it's getting there. I'd even bet that there's a form memo tucked away in every embassy safe that's headed, 'What to Do After the Ambassador's Kidnapped,' so you wouldn't call me in if it were just the simple chore of ransoming the Chicken."

"The what?"

"The Chicken," I said. "That's what they used to call Killingsworth on the paper, because he was. Chicken."

Coors frowned carefully and it may have been the same frown that he employed when the new African ambassador's tart of a wife chose the wrong fork in the Benjamin Franklin State Dining Room. "You weren't exactly our first choice, Mr. St. Ives. You weren't even our second, and if it weren't for the time factor, we would—"

"Why don't you?" I interrupted. "Why not get a bright young Harvard or Yale from one of those ever so discreet Washington–New York–Paris law firms. You know what I mean. The kind with five or six grand old names strung together that probably got its start sixty years ago when it handled one of those banana revolutions for you and United Fruit down in South America. They don't charge much. Not more than ten or fifteen times what I do and nobody's ever complained about their manners."

Coors hooded his eyes again. "You think you're an extremely clever person, don't you?" he said and managed to make person sound like son of a bitch. But there was no venom in his tone despite the reptilian look. There was only a kind of resigned weariness as if his lot in life were to put up with an endless series of jaspers who felt that they were extremely clever sons of bitches.

"I only asked a question," I said.

"I know you did. You want to know why we picked wonderful you. First of all, you were logical because you've had a measure of experience in this kind of business."

"It's how I make a living."

"Secondly, you could become readily available."

"That only took the threat of a Congressional investigation," I said. "I liked that. You had to have someone who'd lose if he said no, so whoever remembered me and the African shield fiasco must have gone around chuckling about it all morning."

"The last, but not least of our considerations, is that you're an outsider and as such will have a controlled, strictly limited access to others in the department."

"How's that an advantage?" I said.

"Security," Coors said.

"You don't trust your own kind?"

"Not with this."

"What about the CIA? There're days when they don't talk much. Fridays, I think."

"It's our own dirty linen," Coors said and looked mildly pleased with the cryptic flavor of the worn phrase.

"How dirty?"

"Filthy."

"What makes you so sure I won't gossip down at the corner laundromat?" I said, poking a flicker of life into the dying analogy.

"If you did," Coors said slowly, "you might find yourself in a rather embarrassing position." He shook his head decisively. "No, you won't ever talk about our dirty linen, Mr. St. Ives."

"I'll ask again. Why?"

The smile that he gave me had a fine chill in it which fully matched the snow and slush outside. "You won't talk about it," he said, "because before you're done, you'll be wearing it."

CHAPTER 2

It had all started the day before in one of those cold, drafty halls that you can hire by the hour over on West Thirty-ninth Street and the canvas banner that hung above the platform spelled out CHEAPAR in fat Gothic letters and also portrayed a cuddly-looking rat with mellow blue eyes.

The audience consisted of nearly three-dozen men and women whose common denominator was a warm, misty expression and a prosperous, even rich appearance. I estimated that at least three of them had yet to celebrate their sixty-fifth birthdays.

The audience just escaped being outnumbered by members of the New York press who, as usual, had nothing either warm or misty about their expressions. We had drawn three local television news teams, four radio reporters, three photographers, a brace of wire service men, and accredited representatives from the *Times,* the *Daily News,* the *Post,* and *The Village Voice. The Wall Street Journal* had failed to show.

Myron Greene, the lawyer, crept into the hall and carefully chose a rear seat just as our chairman pro tem, Henry Knight, broke down and had to be led away sobbing, overcome by his own vivid account of the death screams that escape from the throats of furry little bodies that have just nibbled at poison.

At forty-three, Henry Knight was still much in demand for juvenile leads on and off Broadway, but his finest performance may well have been that Monday afternoon in February as he huddled in the folding metal chair, his handsome, ageless face buried in a handkerchief, his body wracked by uncontrollable sobs. Or laughter. He got a warm round of appreciative, even sympathetic applause from everyone in the audience but Myron Greene, the lawyer, and for a moment I worried lest Knight rise to take his bows.

From the way his wheezes had rasped over the phone earlier that day I could tell that Myron Greene had been either angry or excited. Probably both. His asthma never bothered him when he talked to other clients. But then he could scarcely afford to get angry with six- and seven-hundred-million-dollar conglomerates, and the only excitement they ever supplied came but once or twice a year, if that often, when the Justice Department threatened an antitrust suit or two.

Nodding slightly at Greene, who refused to nod back, I moved quickly to the podium and informed the audience, now even more misty-eyed than ever, that because our temporary chairman's sensitive nature precluded him from continuing, we would next hear from the founder and executive director of CHEAPAR, Park Tyler Wisdom III, who presumably was made of stronger stuff. That earned another round of applause from the audience, a faint cheer from the press, and an impatient, exasperated glare from Myron Greene.

Wisdom must have been all of thirty then, round of face, merry of eye, and possessed of that beaming confidence which comes from having inherited a seven-million-dollar trust fund from grandma at twenty-two. He had doffed his usual attire of sweat shirt and army surplus trousers in favor of a swallowtail coat, striped pants, a gray double-breasted vest, and a wing collar garnished by a plum-colored cravat. All in all, he looked very much like the slightly overweight second secretary of some pre-World War II Balkan embassy. The faintly tinted pince-nez that he wore did nothing to spoil the effect.

Waving the pince-nez around, Wisdom made a stirring five-minute pitch for contributions and succeeded in securing pledges that totaled nearly $1500. A few wrote checks on the spot. I moved over to him, whispered into his ear, and he beamed once more and held up his arms for attention.

"Mr. Philip St. Ives, our public relations secretary, informs me that CHEAPAR's volunteer legal counsel has just arrived." Wisdom pointed to the rear of the hall. "Could we have a nice round of applause for Mr. Myron Greene?" Old necks craned, arthritic hands clapped, and lined faces smiled and bobbed their greetings at Myron Greene who, looking completely miserable, did manage a half wave at the audience and a glare of sheer malevolence at me.

I was Myron Greene's client chiefly because at thirty-six he still dreamed of becoming a flashy criminal lawyer or a gentleman racing car driver or an international trouble-shooter or almost anything other than what he was: an extremely successful corporation attorney with offices on Madison, a home in Darien, and a 475-horsepower Shelby Cobra that he got to drive on weekends if he promised the wife and kids not to go over sixty-five.

By having me as a client, Greene mistakenly believed that he injected an occasional dose of excitement, intrigue, and God knows what else into what he considered to be his otherwise staid life. And if he usually had to pay for it with asthma, annoyance, and even anger, he seemed to feel that it was well worth the price and I was too diffident to tell him that it wasn't.

Earlier in the day, Myron Greene had called and tried to explain, in between wheezes, that he had to see me immediately, within the hour—sooner, if possible. I'd interrupted him to ask, "You ever call that doctor I recommended?"

"What doctor?"

"The specialist in psychosomatic disorders."

"My asthma is not a psychosomatic disorder and I resent your—"

"Calm down, Myron," I'd said. "Take a deep breath."

"Damn it," he'd said, "what I have to see you about is important."

"So is my meeting."

Myron Greene had been silent for several moments. Not even a wheeze. He could have been counting to ten—or perhaps twenty. "All right," he'd said finally, "how long does this circus of yours last?"

"Thirty minutes, I think. Maybe forty-five."

"Well, I have to go downtown around four. I suppose I could stop by. Where is it again?"

I'd given him the address and he'd wheezed as he wrote it down. I assumed that he wrote it down. "This is the most childish—the most juvenile—"

"No, it isn't, Myron."

"If it's not juvenile, what do you call it?"

"A noble cause," I'd said and hung up.

Wisdom was explaining that we were holding a combination membership meeting and press conference and that he would now entertain questions from the press. If he couldn't answer them, he was sure that Mr. St. Ives could, or perhaps Mr. Knight, providing that the chairman pro tem had recovered sufficiently from his emotional ordeal.

The man from the CBS television station was up first. Wisdom acknowledged him with a grand wave of the pince-nez. "Mr. Wisdom," he said, "could you explain once more for our viewers just what CHEAPAR stands for?"

"Delighted," Wisdom said. "CHEAPAR is an acronym which stands for the Committee for Humane Extermination of All Park Avenue Rats."

The *Daily News* wanted to know what was so special about Park Avenue rats. It was one of the questions that Wisdom was waiting for.

"You must understand," he said with another fine flourish of the pince-nez, "that only recently have rats invaded Park Avenue. A number of residents there complained. I did so myself—as did most, if not all, of the ladies and gentlemen here today. This is understandable."

He put the pince-nez back on his nose and started jabbing at the air with a forefinger. "I want to make it perfectly clear that CHEAPAR is no organization of bleeding hearts. We well recognize that rats, through no fault of their own, are often the carriers of dread disease.

"But," he said, taking off the pince-nez and again holding it up for emphasis, "no sooner had our complaints been lodged than the city responded with what can only be described as terrifying alacrity. The Park Avenue rats were singled out for mass slaughter by the most barbaric means— as Mr. Knight tried to tell you before he was overcome by the horror of his own description."

Wisdom paused to give Knight a benign look and Knight let the audience have another glance at his profile before he ducked it back into his handkerchief.

The *Post* reporter wanted to know what Wisdom suggested. "Decompression," he answered quickly. "The rats should be captured alive in cagelike traps and then put to sleep in a chamber from which the air is almost instantaneously removed. The method is recommended by many humane societies. It's quick and painless—just like taking a nice, long nap." That got another fine round of applause from the audience. I noticed that Myron Greene now held his head in his hands.

A wire service reporter asked if CHEAPAR planned to limit its operations to the rats on Park Avenue.

"Certainly," Wisdom answered with some asperity.

When the wire service man wanted to know why, Wisdom replied, "Because Park Avenue rats—and I don't make this charge lightly—but Park Avenue rats are the only ones being discriminated against by the City of New York."

Well, that was the lead and they all knew it and, as usual, they went along with Wisdom who could be counted on to brighten their day about seven or eight times a year. The girl from *The Village Voice*, struggling to keep a straight face, asked, "Can you explain what form this discrimination against Park Avenue rats takes as opposed, say, to the rats of Harlem or Greenwich Village or Bedford-Stuyvesant?"

"Indeed I can," Wisdom said. "Take your average rat in Harlem. Nobody bothers him, particularly not the City. He's left alone as long as he stays in Harlem. But let him try to improve his lot, let him try to move downtown to Park Avenue, and the vicious, discriminatory rat control forces are unleashed. He is clubbed, poisoned, and there is even talk of using—yes, there is! There are those who would use gas!" That produced a sharp chorus of no's from the audience and another faint cheer from the press. Myron Greene was now slumped back in his chair, staring at the dirty ceiling. Knight whimpered a couple of times.

The *Times* man gave up a valiant battle to maintain his grave expression and asked, "Do you think, Mr. Wisdom, that politics or pressure may have caused this—uh—discrimination?"

"Possibly, sir, possibly. Thus far, we have had no complaints of rat brutality from any area other than Park Avenue. We of course hope that this is not a political football, but nevertheless we have asked Mr. St. Ives to investigate."

"How about it, Phil?" the man from the *Post* asked.

I rose and nodded in what I hoped was a somber fashion. "Our preliminary survey," I said, "indicates that both politics and pressure have played no small part in the discriminatory brutalization of Park Avenue rats. We're preparing a White Paper on this and I hope to have copies of it to you within the next few days."

There was a muffled groan from the rear that came from Myron Greene who had his head back in his hands.

After several more questions the man from the *Times* said, "Thank you, Mr. Wisdom," and the press conference was over. The superannuated audience, representing a collective net worth of around a half-billion dollars, rose creakily and crowded about Wisdom and Knight to congratulate one and comfort the other.

I walked to the rear to find out what Myron Greene considered so important that he would stop off at a hired hall on his way downtown. After listening for ten minutes, I agreed that it might be important, even vital, but told him that I wasn't interested. It took him another fifteen minutes to tell me why I was.

CHAPTER **3**

There had been a time, nearly five years ago, when I might have been sitting in that rented hall on Thirty-ninth Street with the rest of the press, feeding lines to Wisdom and Knight, more or less serving as an accommodating shill for their put-on.

But then it had been my job to write a column five times a week for a now defunct and largely unmourned newspaper about the cards and cautions who infest New York. I had developed a breezy, perhaps irreverent style, the source material had been limitless, the hours flexible, and I found myself with a respectable readership and inexplicably the trust and confidence of a swarm of thieves, cops, hustlers, high rollers, con men, prophets, assorted saviors, bums, middle echelon Mafiosi, and people who seemed to spend most of their time hanging around telephone booths waiting for someone to call.

A small-time thief, who proudly described himself as Constant Reader, had stolen a goodly amount of jewelry from one of Myron Greene's clients and then informed the lawyer that he was perfectly willing to sell it all back at nominal cost providing that I served as the go-between. I had done so because it provided material for a couple of fair columns that appeared just before the newspaper folded on Christmas Eve, a date much favored by publishers to suspend operations, possibly because of the attendant poignancy, but more probably because few persons really give a damn about reading a newspaper on Christmas Day.

Just as the last of my severance pay was running out three months later, I again was approached by Myron Greene, this time to serve as the intermediary or payoff man in the kidnapping of the son of a client of a fellow attorney who recalled how I had handled the jewelry thing. So for $10,000 in what Greene, to my dismay, insisted on calling "danger money," I traded a satchel stuffed with $100,000 for the missing heir who, I felt—once we became acquainted—should have stayed missing.

The third time around I became Myron Greene's client. He now negotiated my fees in exchange for ten percent of whatever I earned. He also reluctantly agreed to perform a few personal chores such as handling my divorce (his first and last such case), dispatching my alimony payments, paying my bills, and seeing to it that my quarterly income tax statements were filed on time. Since it couldn't possibly have been the money that interested him, I decided that he harbored a sneaking admiration for the thieves, rogues, and mountebanks that I palled around with and it was a charge he never bothered to deny.

I found it to be a trade that needed neither advertising nor a hard-hitting publicity campaign. Word of mouth did nicely. Thieves who got caught recommended me to fellow inmates who were soon to be released. Insurance companies recommended me to their customers and to rival firms. Lawyers recommended me to other lawyers and sometimes even the police would damn me with a grudging bit of faint praise. "Well, he's as honest as you could expect." That sort of thing.

So if I didn't quite prosper, I at least survived, sometimes going south in the winter and to Europe in the spring or fall, content with the three or four or even five assignments that came my way during a year and always sympathetic when each of them brought on another of Myron Greene's asthma attacks.

The rest of the time I read, went to the films in the morning, played table stakes poker, chased and even caught a few girls, fed stray dogs and cats and the pigeons in Central Park, visited the galleries and some friendly bars, showed up at all parades, joined a few respectable demonstrations, and some not so respectable, took magazines and cigarettes to jailed thieves whom I'd done business with, dropped out of group therapy after one disastrous session, and sometimes just sat around in my "deluxe" efficiency apartment on the ninth floor of the Adelphi on East Forty-sixth Street and stared at the wall.

So it really wasn't until the young thing from the *Daily News* called some four years after my own paper had folded and requested an interview that I realized I'd become, willy-nilly, one of those about whom I used to write: a social deviant, a professional pariah, even, for God's sake, a character.

I had recently returned from Washington where I had almost bungled a job that had involved the theft of a priceless brass shield, a couple of feuding African nations, and the international oil crowd. Some people had been killed, one had

25

been arrested with the shield in Rotterdam, and another was still sulking because he thought he had been cheated out of a few billion dollars' worth of oil.

The young thing from the *Daily News* wanted to know all about the go-between calling, remarked that I must live a fascinating life, ate six brownies (the young today are constantly famished), and then trotted off to write up the lies I'd told her.

I called Myron Greene. "No more," I said.

"No more what?"

"No more international stuff. No more African colonels with big warm smiles and greedy little lies. No more State Department types. No more dead bodies, imported or domestic. No more—"

"I thought we handled it all quite well, everything considered," he said.

"You think we did?" I said, bearing down hard on the *we* only to notice that it flitted right by him.

"Yes, as a matter of fact, I do. I've already made arrangements with the museum for your fee to be paid in full."

"They must have liked that," I said.

"Not really; not after I pointed out that a lawsuit could prove most embarrassing to all concerned."

"Let's keep it simple from now on, Myron. You know. The purloined necklace, the missing bearer bonds, the stolen securities, even the kidnapped company comptroller. They're more in line with whatever talents I have to offer. An international diddle isn't."

"We've never had a kidnapped company comptroller," he said with all the earnest literalness of his profession.

"If we do, let's make sure he's a local boy. Or even a du

Pont from Delaware. But no more international trade. They're not at all keen on following the rules."

"Very well, if you insist," he said a little stiffly, I felt, as if making a note to send me a white feather that afternoon. "But I think you should admit that the entire affair was fascinating."

"Fascinating," I said, hung up, and tried to recall the exact day that an incurable romantic had been foisted on me as lawyer, business manager, and principal source of income. I wanted to mark it off on the calendar as a date not to remember.

So now we stood there in the rear of that drafty, rented hall which had seen ten thousand meetings held and ten thousand committees formed and perhaps fifty thousand resolutions passed, all for or against something that no longer mattered to anyone, while I listened to Myron Greene explain why I had to be in an office on the third floor of the State Department in Washington the following day.

When he finished, I said, "I told you no more international stuff, Myron."

"But you know him," he said. "And they know that you know him."

"That was a long time ago. I didn't like him even then and it was a fully reciprocated feeling."

"He hired you," Greene said. "He gave you your very first job."

"And fired me. From my very first job."

Myron Greene was silent for a moment as he carefully undid and then refastened the six leather-covered buttons on his heather tweed Norfolk jacket that I hoped wouldn't shake the confidence of whomever he was seeing downtown. When he was through fooling with his jacket he smoothed back his blond hair whose length would draw no stares on Madison, but might earn a disapproving glance from a Superior Court judge, providing Greene ever ventured into a courtroom, which he had done only twice during the five years that I'd known him. Myron Greene's clients, but for me, weren't the kind who were hailed into court.

"Well, I'm afraid that you'll have to keep the appointment in any event," he said and directed a stubborn stare past my shoulder. I turned to see what was so fascinating but it was only Wisdom and Henry Knight chuckling at each other as they took down the CHEAPAR banner. The audience and the press had gone.

"Why?" I said.

"Because they want to explain it to you personally."

"Tell them to call me."

"I told them you'd be there at eleven. Tomorrow."

"Now you can tell them that I won't."

"Sorry, but it's either-or now."

"Either-or what?"

"Either you show up in Washington at eleven tomorrow or a federal marshal serves you here with a subpoena at noon." His stubborn stare turned on me and now it was corporation lawyer Greene informing the executive board that there was nothing to be done but file bankruptcy proceedings and yes, it was a damned shame about all those widow and orphan stockholders.

"Subpoena for what?" I said.

Myron Greene smiled slightly. "For Congressman Royker's subcommittee."

"Royker's a fool."

"Even a fool can open up a can of worms," Greene said wisely.

"What can?"

"He could start poking into what really happened to the shield and the Africans and the oil crowd. He's good at things like that as long as they produce headlines. And the headlines should be interesting, but you'd know more about that than I would."

"You were supposed to have fixed it," I said. "You were supposed to have gone around with dustpan and whisk broom and tidied it all up."

Myron Greene smiled again. It was broader this time, almost friendly. I also noticed that he was no longer wheezing. "Oh, I did," he said. "I told them that you'd be there."

I walked over to the door and gazed down the long flight of stairs. If I hurried, I could be in Mexico tomorrow. Guadalajara perhaps; that had a nice ring. Instead, I turned and went slowly back to Myron Greene.

"How much are the kidnappers asking?"

"For the ambassador?"

"For the Chicken."

"Is that what you called him?"

"We did when he was managing editor. I don't know what they called him when he got to be publisher. He'd fired me by then."

"A million dollars."

"You didn't say it right, Myron. There wasn't enough reverence in your tone and that means that there's not going to be any ten percent."

He nodded.

"Five?" I said without much hope.

He shook his head this time. "Three," he said, "and I had to press for that."

"Hard?"

"Very hard."

"State must not think he's worth a million either," I said. "How long have they had him?"

"Since day before yesterday. Saturday."

"Another day or two and whoever's got him will make State an offer to take him back."

"I don't think so," Myron Greene said.

"You don't know him."

"The kidnappers are demanding something more."

"What?"

"Not what. Who."

"All right. Who?"

"Anton Pernik. The poet."

"He's in jail."

"House arrest really."

"I never could read him."

"He won the Nobel Prize," Myron Greene said.

"So did Sinclair Lewis and I can't read him either."

"Well?" Myron Greene asked.

"I don't know anyone in Belgrade."

"It didn't happen in Belgrade," he said. "It happened in Sarajevo."

"It sometimes does," I said, "but I don't know anyone there either."

"The Yugoslav government has expressed its willingness to cooperate."

"They'll give up Pernik?"

"Yes."

"They probably can't read him either."

"Your services were requested, of course."

"By whom, Killingsworth?"

"No," he said and smiled again, even more broadly than before. Myron Greene was enjoying himself. "Not by the ambassador. By Anton Pernik."

"Maybe I'll try to read him again," I said.

CHAPTER 4

Amfred Killingsworth had been managing editor of
the *Chicago Post* only six months in 1957 before *Who's Who*
got around to sending him a form letter that contained a request for a brief life history along with the usual hard sell
pitch to buy the 1958 edition at a sizable discount.

Killingsworth ordered a dozen copies and then used four
8½" x 11" sheets, single-spaced, to tell all about himself and
the high points of his life, beginning with the American
Legion oratory prize of five dollars that he won in 1932 when
he was eleven and in Miss Nadine Cooper's 6-A class at
Horace Mann school in Omaha. I know because he gave me
his own draft to boil down to three pages.

"Four pages is just a shade too long, don't you think?" he
said in that deep butterscotch voice of his that made "please
pass the salt" sound even better than the first line in *Moby
Dick*.

"I don't know," I said, rolling a sheet of paper into my
typewriter, "you've led a rather fulsome life."

32

I'm not sure why I bothered to play my word games with Killingsworth because all he'd said was, "Yes," nodded his big, square, blond head in thoughtful agreement, and added, "I guess that's the right word for it." Then he'd started to leave, but turned back to say, "By the way, if you can't boil me down to three pages, Phil, three and a half will do just fine."

I think the only person with more space in *Who's Who* the following year was Douglas MacArthur.

Killingsworth had been thirty-seven when he was named managing editor of the *Post* and his autobiography (which modesty kept him from writing until he was forty) could have been called *I Was There, Charlie,* because he had been. Instead, he called it *The Killingsworth Story* and it sold 619 copies. An untroubled cynic on the *Post* once remarked that the only thing Killingsworth had missed during World War II was the line at an Army induction center.

He had been at Pearl Harbor, of course, on December 7, 1941. He was on his way back from the Moral Rearmament oratorical finals for college seniors in Manila and when the attack came, Killingsworth was delivering an abbreviated fifteen-minute version of his speech over a Honolulu radio station. After the staff announcer panicked, a quick-thinking engineer hustled Killingsworth up to the roof, handed him a microphone, and told him to start talking. He was good at that and so by shortwave Amfred Killingsworth gave one of the first eyewitness accounts of the Japanese attack, describing everything he saw and a hell of a lot of what he imagined—such as the Japanese landing at Waikiki.

An hour after the radio networks had transcribed and rebroadcast his description in the states, Killingsworth received six job offers. He picked the one from the *Chicago Post* because his father had bought it every Sunday morning for seventeen years on the strength of its comic section.

After that, Amfred Killingsworth's by-line topped warm, often soggy human interest stories from Corregidor, New Caledonia, Guadalcanal, Washington, North Africa, London, Normandy, Leyte Gulf, Chungking, Iwo Jima, Rome, Rheims, Berlin, and from aboard the U.S.S. *Missouri* on September 2, 1945. He usually managed to get either a dog or a cat into his stories.

When the war ended, Killingsworth was made editorial page editor of the *Post* where it really didn't matter whether he could write or even spell. He was twenty-five years old. A year later, with his eye on his future if not on his bride, he married Norma, the thirty-three-year-old daughter of Obadiah Singleton, editor and publisher of the *Post*. Singleton was then seventy-three and obsessed with his antivivisection crusade, his paper's annual National Junior Wrestling Tournament, the Communist conspiracy (both international and domestic), the machinations of Wall Street, and the welfare of his daughter—in just about that order. Norma suffered occasional mild seizures, endured a bad case of postadolescent acne, and lusted after bellhops, delivery men, cab drivers, and bartenders. "The best time to catch her," a cab driver had once told a mildly interested *Post* reporter, "is when she goes into that fit. I mean it's a real tough ride."

Killingsworth quickly got his new bride with child and then left for a three-year assignment in Europe as roving correspondent. He especially liked to cover the tulip festival in Holland. When he came back to Chicago, he again took over the editorial page and that's where he stayed until one night in early 1957 when old man Singleton wandered down to the city room and found the managing editor drunk. He wasn't as drunk as usual, but Singleton couldn't tell the difference, so he fired him. When he was through with that, he turned to three reporters and a rewrite man and fired them for, as he later put it, "just standing around gawking."

The next day Singleton named his son-in-law managing editor and three days later Killingsworth hired me to replace one of the fired reporters. He'd said, "I like the cut of your jib, St. Ives; welcome aboard," and thus acquired himself a lifelong enemy.

There was no reason to tell Hamilton Coors any of this as we sat in the third-floor State Department office that seemed to belong to no one in particular. I was watching it snow; Coors was watching me watch. Neither of us had said anything for twenty or thirty seconds.

"Tell me more about the dirty linen," I said finally.

"Killingsworth's a fool, of course," Coors said without rancor, but not without a trace of sadness.

"How do the Yugoslavs rate him?"

"Unofficially, they've asked that he be recalled."

"Are their complaints general or specific?" I said. "Or both?"

Coors's eyes left me and wandered around the room, but there wasn't much to see, so they finally settled on the flag. "Do you remember Alexander Rankovic?"

"Just the name," I said. "He was once something or other in the Yugoslav government."

"Vice-president," Coors said, "until five or six years ago when Tito kicked him out."

"I remember now, but I don't remember why."

"Rankovic wasn't only vice-president, he was also head of the UDBA, its secret police."

"Well, they did give him something to do."

Coors frowned and said, "Mmmm," to let me know that he didn't regard my remark as substantive. "There were charges and even countercharges for a while," he said, "but the real blowup came when Tito claimed to have found a hidden microphone in his own house."

"That could well cause a rift."

From behind closed lips Coors gave his opinion of my remark with another "Mmmm," and then said, "Rankovic was charged, stripped of his public office, and finally forced into obscurity. He was never tried publicly."

"Then what?"

"Rankovic had a confidential assistant who'd been with him since the war. His name is Jovan Tavro. What Rankovic knew as head of the secret police, Tavro also knew. A few weeks ago, Tavro started to meet secretly with Killingsworth."

"Who never could keep anything to himself."

"He didn't tell us."

"Who did."

"The Yugoslavs. It upset them so much that they became, well, insistent about Killingsworth's recall."

"But he got kidnapped before you could fetch him home."

Coors hooded his eyes again and once more sent them wandering around the room in search of something to light on. He had to settle for the flag again. "Not exactly," he said finally.

"What do you mean not exactly?"

"We recalled him immediately."

"And?"

"Killingsworth refused to leave," he said in a voice so low that he almost mumbled it, as though hoping that I wouldn't bother to listen.

"Amfred Woodrow Killingsworth," I said, "Ambassador Extraordinary and Plenipotentiary as well as Dunce Designate. Let me guess why he refused to leave. He's in the thick of a monarchist plot to restore Peter to the throne?"

"No," Coors said.

"It's worse?"

He paused for a long time as though he were silently trying out some phrases to determine how bad they would sound when he finally had to say them. "Jovan Tavro was in possession of information that could be extremely valuable to whoever possessed it."

"And Killingsworth's now got it."

Coors said nothing. It was, I suppose a diplomatic silence.

"So Killingsworth is blackmailing you." Coors blinked his eyes at that.

"Either you keep him on as ambassador, or he'll spread Tavro's information all over page one of the *Chicago Post* under a copyrighted by-line."

Coors sighed. "You left out his syndicated news service."

"And you've left out something," I said.

"Oh?"

"You've left out why Killingsworth really doesn't want to come home."

"That," Coors said.

"That," I said.

For the first time a really pained expression appeared on his dour face. It was a look that could have been caused by either acute embarrassment or a sudden migraine attack. They both hurt. He gently massaged his temples with the tips of his fingers, looking at the top of his desk.

"He won't come back," he said to the desk top, spacing each word carefully, "because he says he's in love."

Well, it can happen at fifty as easily as at fifteen, but it wasn't at all what I'd expected so I got up and walked across the room to where the picture of the flag hung. I counted the stars and there were still fifty of them. Then I counted the stripes and felt relieved when there were only thirteen. But since it was a State Department flag, I counted them again to be sure.

"He's in love with a slinky Eurasian from the Hanoi embassy," I said to the flag.

Coors's voice seemed tired when he spoke. "We could handle that," he said.

"Who does he think he's in love with other than the face he shaves every morning?"

"With Anton Pernik's granddaughter."

"She must be either pretty or sexy, because she couldn't be smart. Not if she's fooling around with Killingsworth."

"She keeps house for Pernik—looks after him," Coors said.

I sat down again and looked at Coors who once more was giving his fingernails a close inspection. First the right hand, then the left.

"How old's the girl?" I said.

"Twenty-two."

"You don't need me. You need some agony column writer. Someone like Ann Landers. When do you let the press in on the kidnapping?"

"This afternoon," Coors said.

"What do the Yugoslavs say?"

"They've agreed to free Pernik."

"What if you don't?" I said.

"Don't what?"

"Don't hand over the million and Pernik."

38

Coors merely shrugged and looked somewhere else. At the flag probably.

"What does that mean?" I said. "That they'd kill Killingsworth?"

"They could threaten to," he said.

"But you'd figure it for a bluff?"

"I'm sure it would be."

"Call it then," I said. "You can't possibly lose."

Coors's large eyes deserted the flag and darted quickly around the room as if in desperate search of some less hallowed place to light. But finally they gave up and once more settled on the flag. It may have given him reassurance or even a sense of purpose. He seemed to need one. "We can't do that," he said and there was only finality in his tone.

"Why not?"

"Because," he said and chewed on his lower lip before continuing. "Because we are the kidnappers."

CHAPTER 5

I was halfway to the door before Coors spoke again and when he did, it stopped me in midstride. It was only one word, but nobody had used it yet and probably wouldn't again because they thought it cost too much. Coors said, "Please."

I turned and said, "Was it yours originally?"

He shook his head. "Not mine. They gave it to me to finish. They do that sometimes."

"There's no million dollars."

"No," he said.

"No ransom demand."

"It's false," he said.

"Faked, just like the snatch."

"Killingsworth doesn't think so. He thinks it's real. So do the Yugoslavs."

"Who pulled it?" I said.

"They're from Trieste. A pair of them."

"Italian or Yugoslavian?"

"Half and half. They won't talk to anyone. They can't afford to."

"What about the girl?" I said.

"She goes with her grandfather."

"Then what?"

"You furnish them with the documents that'll get them out of Yugoslavia and to the States."

"And Killingsworth?"

"With her here, he won't want to stay there. He's in love, remember? When he returns for consultation, he'll be allowed to resign. Quietly."

"What about Pernik?"

"What about him?"

"What happens to him?"

There was only indifference in Coors's voice. "I suppose we'll give him a house out in Hyattsville and he can write some more poetry."

"And the girl?"

"If Killingsworth balks, she goes back to Yugoslavia."

"It's neat," I said. "Someday I'd like to meet him."

"Who?"

"Whoever dreamed this up."

"His name's hardly a household word."

"Neither is shit in some households."

Coors did frown at that, but erased it quickly and asked, "Shall we get on with it?"

"All right."

"When you arrive in Belgrade you'll be met by someone from our embassy. As far as the embassy knows, you're exactly what you are, Philip St. Ives, professional go-between whose services have been requested by Anton Pernik."

"That's a bit thin, even for someone like Myron Greene who dotes on things like that."

Coors's tone grew starchy. "Your Mr. Greene has a strong streak of patriotism which I found rather admirable."

"You mean naive, don't you?" I said. "If Pernik did ask for me, it was only because you had someone tell him to. But Myron doesn't expect you to lie. I do."

I suffered through Coors's glare until he continued. "Your embassy escort will take you to the proper Yugoslav authorities who'll furnish you with the pieces of paper necessary to permit Pernik and his granddaughter to leave the country. Then the kidnappers will contact you and you'll set up the place for the exchange. The Yugoslavs have agreed not to interfere in any way. After the exchange, you escort Killingsworth back to the embassy and we'll take over from there."

"And that's all?" I said.

Coors rested the palms of his hands flat on the desk and looked at me steadily. "Yes. That's all."

"There must be something else—an odd loose end or two."

"No."

"Haven't you forgotten someone?"

"Who?"

"Jovan Tavro. You know, the aide to the deposed vice-president. The one who had all the embarrassing information."

"No," Coors said. "I haven't forgotten him."

"Isn't he in some kind of trouble?" I said. "I don't think Tavro would voluntarily hand anything over to Killingsworth unless he was in trouble. Nobody who knew Killingsworth for five minutes would tell him anything either important or confidential, unless he was desperate. So Tavro must be desperate—almost as desperate as you."

I watched Coors as he increased the pressure of his palms on the desk. "I'm not sure that I follow you," he said in a special tone that he might have been saving for some Senate investigating committee.

I shook my head. "You follow me fine," I said. "You're even a bit ahead of me and your only mistake has been in estimating my catch-up time."

"Really, St. Ives—"

I rose and leaned over the desk toward him, trying to keep most of it out of my voice, but not succeeding too well.

"What the hell do you think I've been doing for the past five years? And who do you think I've done it with, a clutch of choir boys? I've dealt with thieves, Coors, the professional kind who'll lie and cheat and sometimes kill just as quickly as they'll steal, and they'll steal anything that'll bring a dollar and even things that won't. So I've had to outthink them at their own line because every last one of them has wanted to steal something and sell back nothing. The only reason they didn't is that I somehow stayed one jump ahead of them which isn't as easy as it sounds because a lot of them were smart. Even clever. That's not bragging. That's just how I make a living off professional thieves, who're as rotten a bunch as you can find, but there's not one of them who'd even dream of trying to con me with the crap you've been pushing here this morning."

Coors sat through it all patiently enough and even looked as if he had listened to part of it. When I was through and sitting back down and smoking another cigarette, he locked his hands behind his head and regarded the ceiling.

"I told them, of course," he said.

"Told who?"

"Upstairs."

43

"What?"

"That you'd tumble, that it was all too thin without Tavro."
Coors sighed at the ceiling. "They wanted to wait."

"Until when?"

"Until you got there."

"They were wrong."

"Yes, they were, weren't they?" Coors quit looking at the
ceiling and used his fingertips to massage his temples again.
"I've told you no lies. Tavro did go to Killingsworth. He
thought Killingsworth might help him, but Killingsworth instead used the information he got from him to pressure us.
When love comes late in life to some men, it often affects
their judgment. It's affected Killingsworth's."

"So he was kidnapped," I said.

"Only because we couldn't trust him. Would you?"

"Not far," I said.

Coors's palms were back on the desk again, but they no
longer tried to press through it. "By using the Pernik girl
and her grandfather as bait we get Killingsworth back to the
States and that problem is resolved—no doubt a little melo-
dramatically, but melodrama is often no small part of diplo-
macy." He paused and seemed to think about what he had
just said and for a moment I half expected him to jot it down.

"That still leaves us Tavro," I said. "Why didn't you get
him out?"

Coors gave me a thin, almost bitter little smile. "Some forget, I'm afraid, that the Department of State is a large and
cumbersome bureaucracy, perhaps only slightly less wieldy
than that of our friends in the Pentagon across the river. In
such a bureaucracy nothing gets done until it is too late—or
virtually too late. If it is *actually* too late, then obviously

nothing should be done and the bureaucracy sighs its collective relief and returns to its beloved routine."

Coors paused to give me another small, wintry smile. "In Tavro's case, we are only virtually too late, and through a process of pain with which I won't bore you, a course of action has been decided upon. In a bureaucracy such as State, I'm sure you realize, there is nothing more difficult than reaching a decision, unless it is reversing that decision once it has been reached."

"And the decision is to get Tavro out?" I said.

"That's correct."

"How?"

Coors shook his head sorrowfully, as if the star of the spelling bee had just stumbled over Cincinnati. "The decision is not how, Mr. St. Ives, but who."

"Me?"

"Indeed. You."

"How deep am I in?"

Coors looked at his watch, as if it would tell him. "Too deep to get out."

"Because I now know about Killingsworth?"

"That's mostly it."

"What other pressure points have you got besides the Congressional investigation threat—just in case I still say no?"

"Four others."

"As good?"

"Better. Much better."

I nodded and looked out at the snow. It seemed to be coming down even harder than before and somehow that seemed only normal. "So I'm to work it out anyway I can," I said.

"You're to draw upon your extensive experience which, you've given me to understand, has been mostly with thieves.

There's no reason that you shouldn't feel quite at home with us."

"I'll need some help," I said.

Coors didn't like that and he shook his head to prove it. "You can't bring any outsiders into this. I thought I made that plain. They'd never stand for it upstairs."

"They'll have to stand for it," I said. "I'll let you explain why."

"Thank you," he said and drummed the fingers of his left hand on the desk. "Well, I suppose you needn't tell them anything vitally important."

"Such as the truth?"

"Yes," he said. "There's that."

"I'll tell them as little as possible."

"How many?"

"Two."

"Who are they?"

"Let's just use their code names," I said. "One's called Expensive, the other one's Costly."

"Your fee's already been negotiated."

"Negotiations have just been reopened."

"Three percent of a million is thirty thousand dollars," Coors said. "That's a great deal of money for what may not be more than a long weekend."

"I usually get ten percent and I haven't punched a time clock since Chicago."

"Impossible."

"I'll settle for five percent since the million is mythical anyhow. That's my last offer."

"Four," he said.

"In advance."

"What's your bank in New York?"

I told him and he wrote it down. "It'll be deposited to your account tomorrow. You pay your own expenses, of course."

"That's something else I think we should discuss."

"No chance," Coors said and took an envelope from his inside pocket and handed it to me. "An outline is in there plus names, addresses, points of contact, and a suggested timetable."

I put it away and we talked for another three-quarters of an hour until I said, "I think that does it."

Coors glanced over his bare desk as though in search of some scrap of information that might have escaped him. "I don't have anything else unless you have some more questions," he said.

"One," I said. "What if I get into trouble?"

He smiled for the first time in a long while and it may have been the same one he wore when they let him watch the Secretary sign the papers that imposed harsh new economic sanctions on some bankrupt country. "If you get into trouble, Mr. St. Ives," he said, "do drop me a postcard."

A small shivering light-brown man in a thin cotton raincoat got out of a cab at the State Department's green-canopied Twenty-first Street entrance and held the door open for me and then trotted off before I could thank him. The driver twisted around in his seat.

"Now that was a goddamned decent thing of him to do, wasn't it?"

"Very."

"He's from Samoa."

"I was pretty sure he wasn't from around here."

"Where to?"

"The library."

"You mean the Congressional or the main public one?"

"The public one."

He was listed on page 391 of the current Congressional Directory under the Department of State section. First there was the Director of Intelligence and Research and then, thirteen lines down, was Hamilton R. Coors, director, Office of Intelligence for USSR and Eastern Europe.

It said that he lived at 3503 South Whitney Road in MacLean, Virginia, so I wrote it down in case I ever needed to send him a postcard.

CHAPTER **6**

He was about my height, a little over five-feet-eleven, and my weight, 160 or so, and he had my coloring with its sunmissed complexion, and he nearly had my green eyes that some girl had once called sensitive but which my ex-wife had always liked to describe as shifty. His hair also resembled mine in that it still seemed confused about whether to turn dark blond or light brown before it disappeared forever.

If you were slightly nearsighted, without glasses, and perhaps thirty-five feet away, you could have mistaken one of us for the other, but not if you moved much closer because he carried at least ten fewer years than I did and there were those who would have said that he was far better looking. I was one of them.

The snow had followed me back from Washington and I was late arriving. He must have been waiting in the lobby of the Adelphi, but I wasn't aware of him until he approached the desk where I'd stopped to see whether anyone other than the circulation manager of *Time* had bothered to write.

"Mr. St. Ives?" he said to my back.

I turned and said yes, I was St. Ives.

"I am called Artur Bjelo. I wonder if you would be so kind as to spare me a few moments?" His English was precise, as if he'd learned it carefully, but would never be able to get his tongue around the *w*'s.

"What's on your mind?" I said.

He smiled and it came on boyishly, but he may not have been able to help it because he was not much more than twenty-five. I got some minor satisfaction from noticing that my teeth were almost as good as his. "Mr. Anton Pernik," he said and stopped smiling. "He is very much on my mind."

I looked at my mail. It wasn't from *Time* after all. It was from *Harper's*. I put it away in a jacket pocket to savor later.

"Pernik, the poet," I said.

"Yes," he said, "the poet."

"How about a drink?"

"In some private place?"

"The Adelphi bar," I said, "is about as private a place as one can find."

I never thought of the Adelphi as run-down—only neglected by both management and the public. It was primarily a residential hotel patronized by show people, retired brigadier generals and above, their widows, a few of the older call girls, a mysterious gentleman from Karachi, and a host of middle-aged men in dark suits who carried attaché cases, smoked cigars, and talked to each other in the elevator about how the weather was in Miami last week.

I had been living there in a deluxe suite (which meant that it had a Pullman kitchen) for nearly five years, but I had yet to eat a decent meal in its Continental Room whose chef

50

boasted of having smuggled his secret recipes all the way from Bartlesville, Oklahoma.

Still, the bar wasn't bad if you ordered nothing more complicated than a Manhattan. We settled at one of the dark oak tables and I asked for a Scotch and water while Bjelo called for a Margarita which meant that we wouldn't get our drinks for another few minutes because Sid, the bartender, would have to send out for some Tequila. It was that kind of a place.

"What about Pernik?" I said, reaching for a pretzel.

"He is to be exchanged for your ambassador to my country who has been kidnapped." He must have caught my expression because he added quickly, "Already it is on the Associated Press service."

Coors had said the story would be released that afternoon and because of the snow it had taken me three hours to get back to New York so I couldn't find much wrong with the time element. "They have an AP service where you work?" I said.

"At the United Nations," he said.

"The story wouldn't have mentioned my name."

"It did not."

"Are you with the UN itself or with the Yugoslav delegation?"

"I am a very minor and very junior member of the delegation, primarily because of my fluency with languages. Our embassy in Washington naturally informed us immediately that you will serve as the intermediary in the exchange."

"I don't see how this could be an official call then."

"It is entirely unofficial, Mr. St. Ives."

"I see." I didn't, of course, but it was a comment that would help fill the time before the drinks arrived.

"Pernik's granddaughter is to accompany him," he said.

51

"So I understand."

"Do you know her name?"

"Yes."

That didn't stop him from telling me anyway. "Gordana Panić," he said, making the *a* in Panić broad and pronouncing its *c* like the *ch* in church. "Pernik is her maternal grandfather."

The drinks came a few moments later and I noticed that Sid had even salted the rim of the Margarita glass. I offered Bjelo a cigarette, but he shook his head in refusal and drank half of the Margarita. I don't think he noticed the salted rim.

"What's she to you?" I said.

"We were to be married."

"I see," I said again, this time because it's a useful enough phrase when you wish to indicate a sympathetic ear, but not an overactive curiosity.

"We were engaged."

"Mmmm," I said.

"A month ago she tore it off." He looked up quickly from his glass. "Tore is not correct, is it?"

"Broke."

"Yes, broke," he said and finished his drink. "She broke it off."

I couldn't think of any more comforting phrases so I asked Bjelo if he would care for another drink and when he nodded that he would, I signaled to Sid.

"There is another man," Bjelo said.

Ah, Killingsworth, you sly dog.

"An older man," he said.

About twenty-five years older than you and a few million dollars richer. It had to be Killingsworth's money; it couldn't possibly be his personality.

"A friend of yours?" I said.

"No."

"Sometimes it is."

"No, if it were a friend of mine, I would know his name. And if I knew his name, I would kill him."

I studied Bjelo for some indication of sardonic humor or even the hint of overdramatization. There was none. He gazed at me steadily with eyes that I could almost match in color, but not in resolution. He could kill a rival all right, if he got the chance. I decided that it was his Balkan heritage.

"Well, maybe when Miss Panić gets over here you can run down to Washington and patch things up."

Bjelo didn't reply until the second round of drinks was served. "It would be a pleasant world, Mr. St. Ives, if things were so simple."

"They're not, I take it."

"No. I am returning to Yugoslavia shortly—within the week. But I am afraid Gordana will already have gone." He paused. There was nothing for me to say.

"Days are important," he said, frowning into his new drink.

I had nothing to add to that either.

He quit staring into his drink and swallowed half of it. "She would not be coming to this country unless it were for that old fool who is her grandfather. That one lives in the past. Have you read him?"

"Not recently," I said.

"He is the only poet who improves in translation. He is unreadable in Croatian."

"Well, they did give him a Nobel Prize."

"Politics," Bjelo said, almost spitting the word. "He boasts of having tried to make peace between Mihailović's Cetniks and President Tito during the war. But he was a Croat and Mihailović hated Croats worse than he hated Communists. Besides, Pernik was a Royalist and Tito and his Partisans despised Royalists. So the old fool was rebuffed by both sides and because he had nothing else to do, he wrote that disaster of a poem."

"It was called an epic," I said.

Bjelo snorted and used both his mouth and nose to do it. "If ten thousand lines of doggerel can be described as an epic then, yes, that is what it was. But its imagery was fatuous; its narrative redundant; its meter impossible; and its theme naive to the point of mawkishness."

"Apparently, you're something of a critic," I said

He shook his head slowly. "No, Mr. St. Ives," he said and there was nothing but ingenuousness in his tone, "I am something of a poet."

Over the years I have met a number of persons who have described themselves as poets. Some lied when they did it. Some boasted. Some murmured it a little dreamily, some blushed, and some mumbled it as if they hoped I wouldn't hear. But none said it matter of factly, as did Bjelo, and I almost believed him.

"But you're not here to discuss if poetry should be, not mean," I said.

"I'm here to make a request, Mr. St. Ives," he said.

"All right."

"First, I must ask a question."

"All right."

"When will Gordana and her grandfather be exchanged for your ambassador?"

"That's up to the kidnappers," I said. "I have no idea."

"I am going to make a strange request."

"Go ahead."

He looked at me and that hint of resolution was back in his eyes. "I am going to ask you—no, that is too weak a word. I am going to implore you to delay the exchange for one week."

"To stall it," I said.

"Yes, stall it."

"Why?"

"I must see Gordana."

"Write her a letter."

"I have written her dozens. There is no answer."

"Call her."

"She refuses to answer."

"I'm sorry I can't help you," I said.

"You refuse?"

"Yes, if you want to put it that way, I refuse. I'm a go-between, Mr. Bjelo, not Cupid. A man has been kidnapped and you're asking me to postpone his release while you patch up a lovers' quarrel. You don't have a good enough reason. In fact, you don't have much of a reason at all."

"You won't reconsider?" he said. "I ask only for a week."

"No."

He nodded and played with the stem of his empty glass, moving it this way and that. "Then," he said softly, "I have some bad news for you."

"That's the kind I'm most familiar with."

He looked up at me and I realized why I didn't quite believe him when he said he was a poet. Poets don't have eyes like that. "The news is this," he said. "If you go ahead with the exchange without granting me the week's delay, then neither Gordana Panić nor her grandfather will leave Yugo-slavia."

"That's not news," I said. "That's a warning."

He nodded thoughtfully and then rose. "Yes," he said. "It could be called that."

I rose too. "That's all?"

He picked up a tweed topcoat from a chair. "That's all, Mr. St. Ives, except that I believe this is your coat." He handed it to me and picked up the other one which could have been the twin of the one I held. "Yes," he said, "see—yours does not have this rip in its neck." He put the coat on, buttoned it, and looked at me. "I'm sorry if you expected something more dramatic."

"Not at all," I said. "I thought you were swell."

He smiled slightly. "I wish I could thank you for your time, but—" He made a small gesture.

"That's quite all right," I said, damned if he'd win the politeness prize.

"You can reconsider."

"Yes. I can, but I won't."

"That's a pity," he said, turned and walked from the bar. I followed him into the lobby and because I had nothing better to do watched him push through the revolving door, duck his head at the snow, and then pause at the curb before jaywalking Forty-sixth Street.

He stepped out into the street and the white Impala, hitting forty by the time he took three steps, still had to swerve if it were going to do it and that made its rear wheels skid just enough to slow it down and give Bjelo the bare split second that wouldn't have been enough for most people, but seemed plenty for him. He leaped back and to one side and the Impala's right front fender may have brushed him but it didn't stop to find out. The car skidded a little again as its accelerating rear wheels grabbed for purchase in the slush and snow, straightened, and then sped east.

Bjelo didn't bother to look at the disappearing car. He gave his gray tweed coat a perfunctory brush, turned quickly but still calmly, and began walking west at a pace that was little faster than a casual stroll and with the air of a man who finds it pointless to dwell on either near-misses or hits.

I rode the elevator up to my ninth-floor apartment and made a phone call and the young lady with the Yugoslav delegation at the United Nations sounded disappointed when she couldn't connect me with Artur Bjelo because no one of that name had ever worked there.

I made two more phone calls, long ones, and then I stood by the window and looked out at the snow and tried to decide whether the driver of the Impala had been a professional or an amateur. But even professionals can't see too clearly at forty miles per hour in twilight snow because it tends to make all men who are about five-eleven with brownish blond hair and pale complexions and identical topcoats look very much alike.

CHAPTER 7

They both wore belted trench coats and the shorter one had covered his head with a dark blue beret while the taller one sported a high-crowned pale gray fedora with the brim snapped down both fore and aft. They stood near the Pan Am counter at Kennedy International, their eyes protected from the dark February night by sunglasses, and talked to each other without moving their lips like a couple of tired old cons in a prison run by Warner Brothers.

They didn't notice my approach, perhaps because they were both only half-turned toward me, but more likely because neither of them could see much of anything through those wraparound shades. I tapped the shorter one on the left shoulder and said, "Did you remember the detonators, Vladimir?"

Park Tyler Wisdom III turned and beamed. "Ah," he said, "it's Philip St. Ives, known and feared by the scum of two continents."

I looked at Henry Knight who wore the fedora with the toadstool brim. "What the hell are you supposed to be?"

"Hardbitten adventurers, chief," Knight said. "We all dress like this." He paused to frown at my tweed topcoat and hatless head. "Except you," he added.

"I'm the clean-cut one in the trio," I said. "Obviously the leader." I reached into my coat pocket and handed each of them an envelope. "Here're your tickets. It's Pan Am flight two and it's due out at seven. We arrive in Frankfurt at ten-fifteen tomorrow morning and change to JAT flight three fifty-one at twelve forty-five. We land in Belgrade at three twenty-five."

Wisdom looked at his ticket. "On the cheap, I see," he said.

"I thought it would be cozier, three abreast," I said. "Any trouble about your visas?"

Knight shook his head. "They just asked business or pleasure and I said pleasure."

"Let's hope you were right," I said.

It had taken me only eleven minutes to convince Henry Knight that he should come along. It might have taken longer, except that when I called he was in the middle of a fight with Winifred, his tall, leggy wife who looked like a show girl but who wrote and illustrated remarkably tender and successful children's books. When I was about two-thirds of the way through my pitch, Knight had said, "Hold on a second, Phil."

I could hear Winifred yell something at him and, perhaps because he couldn't resist the opportunity, he had yelled back, "Why don't you just write me about it in Belgrade!" Then he returned to the phone with, "When do we leave?" Pride, I long ago found out, often causes the decisions made in the heat of a domestic argument to be just as irrevocable as they are stupid. But Knight's quick decision may have been influenced by the fact that he had been in between plays for eight weeks and Winifred was on a tight deadline and since I was offering all expenses plus double the Equity scale, it probably sounded better than sitting around the house waiting for his agent to call with some fanciful explanation about how Knight had just missed getting on Carson next week. I didn't worry about the domestic spat. After fourteen years of marriage, Henry and Winifred Knight still thought of each other as the world's most interesting person.

Park Tyler Wisdom III, holder of the Silver Star and some Purple Hearts for performing what he had once called "an extraordinary deed of incredible pusilanimity in the face of overestimated odds" while spending two years in Vietnam, was more difficult to convince than Knight. I had to talk twelve minutes, although four of them were spent declining an urgent invitation to join Wisdom and some friends that evening in a planning session whose aim was to deluge the Pentagon with the nation's worn-out ballpoint pens. The idea, it seemed, was to start a nationwide rumor that the military desperately needed the pens for use in some top secret testing project.

"We could use your help, Phil," Wisdom said. "What do you think of 'Pens for the Pentagon'?"

"That should get them a million or so."

"Rumor has it that they need fifty million."

"I've got a dozen or so I'll send tomorrow. What about the trip?"

"How long?"

"Four days, maybe five."

"Winifred's going to let Henry stray?"

"They're in the middle of a fight and she's on a deadline."

"And we'll bring out the poet and his granddaughter?"

"It could change," I said. "You might just be going along for the ride."

"I never could say no to my President," Wisdom said.

"He didn't ask you," I said. "I did."

"Why me?"

"I don't know," I said. "I thought you could use the money."

"You've always worked these go-between things alone before, haven't you?"

"Until now."

"Why the change?"

"I can't be in two places at once and if something happens in the place I'm not in, I need someone who won't panic or who at least is a good enough actor not to show it."

Wisdom was silent for a moment. "And you think I won't panic?"

"No," I said. "I think you're a hell of a good actor."

There was another brief silence and when Wisdom spoke again the gentle self-mockery that was usually in his tone had gone. "Since you seem to know what you're getting, I'll go."

"I know what I'm getting," I said. "That's why I asked you."

"Thanks," he said in that same quiet, thoughtful tone. "I really mean it."

"I know," I said.

Before Wisdom had gone off to Vietnam and his something less than meteoric rise to buck sergeant in the First Air Cavalry division, he had been to all the right schools, starting when he was six, and seemed destined to live the pleasantly well-ordered life of one who, having inherited seven million dollars at twenty-two, had nothing more bothersome to ponder than what to do with the twenty-one million or so that he'll inherit at thirty-five.

After his first one-year tour was over, he signed on for another one. "It was early 1965 then and I honest to God liked it," he once told me. "I liked being Sergeant Wisdom and soldiering and yelling at privates and the rest of it. Even combat. It was neat and tidy and I knew who the hell I was. I was Sergeant Wisdom of the goddamned infantry. It was my own clearly defined niche in a highly structured framework that just happened to be a war."

Then he got hit the second time and while wounded led what was left of his ambushed platoon back through the Vietcong, and in the process killed what later was officially estimated to be 136 of the enemy. "We didn't care if they were VC or not," Wisdom told me. "We killed anything that moved—men, women, children. It didn't matter, we just panicked. When I got back I expected to be court-martialed, but they gave me the Silver Star instead and I couldn't keep a straight face while the Colonel pinned it on so I laughed at him. I've been laughing ever since. It's either that or cry."

Park Tyler Wisdom and his appreciation of the absurd, I'd decided, could be nothing but useful during the next few days.

The flight to Frankfurt was uneventful, except for the twenty-two dollars that Wisdom won from me at gin. We positioned Knight on the aisle seat where his actor's profile assured us of proper attention from the stewardesses, all of whom claimed to have seen his last play.

"Highly doubtful," Knight told us, "since it closed after two performances."

"They're probably thinking of the one before that," Wisdom said.

"It closed after six."

Although the Frankfurt airport seemed to have grown smaller since my last trip there, the beer was still the same, and I was enjoying a half-liter of it when Knight said, "Do you have any relatives here?"

"None that I know of."

"There's a guy at the end of the bar behind you who could almost be your double except that he doesn't yet have your dyspeptic glow."

I didn't turn. "Does he have on a gray topcoat?"

"Yes."

I turned then and used the mirror to look at the end of the bar. When Artur Bjelo's eyes met mine in the mirror they didn't hesitate or flicker in recognition. They just kept on going, not hurriedly, but indifferently, as if they were looking for something more interesting to light on than the face of someone they'd apparently never seen before.

I moved down to the end of the bar and tapped him on the shoulder. "Mr. Bjelo," I said.

He turned at the tap and smiled boyishly and then said something in a language I didn't understand, but assumed to be Serbo-Croatian.

"We met day before yesterday," I said, matching his smile in width, if not in years. "We had a drink or two together and talked about poetry."

He shrugged and smiled again and shook his head helplessly in the universal gesture of apologetic incomprehension.

"You almost got run over," I said.

An Englishman standing next to Bjelo was casually following the abortive dialogue. "I'm afraid he doesn't understand a word you say," he said. "He says he speaks nothing but Serbo-Croatian. I know a bit of it, if you'd like me to tell him something."

"Thank you," I said to the Englishman who rattled something off to Bjelo who nodded and smiled his appreciation.

"Now what would you like me to tell him?" the Englishman asked.

"Tell him he's a goddamned liar," I said, turned, and went back up the bar to my beer.

"Did you know him?" Knight asked me.

"I thought I did, but he thought I didn't. Where's Park?"

"He's gone to buy a cuckoo clock. One of those Black Forest things."

"What for?" I said.

Knight sighed and drank the rest of his beer. "I somehow thought it best not to ask."

"You're probably right," I said.

The three of us were among the first half-dozen passengers to board JAT Flight 351 and after we sat there for nearly thirty-five minutes and nothing moved, Knight turned on his charm and asked the Yugoslav stewardess about the delay.

"We are waiting for a passenger," she said. "It should not be much longer now."

The passenger boarded the plane five minutes later and he didn't seem any more concerned about causing the delay than he had been about telling me in English that his name was Artur Bjelo and denying it in Serbo-Croatian two days later. He sat in the aisle seat nearest the exit and neither read nor slept during the three-and-one-half-hour flight. Neither did I.

Bjelo was the first passenger off when we landed at Surcin International Airport near Belgrade and although I looked for him as we went through customs, he seemed to have already cleared them, possibly because he had nothing to declare, not even any more lies.

CHAPTER 8

After we got through customs I started looking around for something young and about six feet tall in a nicely tailored dark suit whose center vent might be a full fourteen inches but whose lapels wouldn't be wide enough to cause any stir at the embassy's annual Fourth of July tea and fireworks do.

I was looking for something male with a slightly superior, world-weary expression who couldn't quite hide his irritation at having been assigned to meet us at the airport, and who could rattle off instructions to the baggage handlers in fluent Serbo-Croatian which he'd picked up in six weeks or so because he had a sponge for a brain and languages came just ever so easy for him.

That's what I was looking for out of prejudice or propaganda or both, so when I got jabbed in the ribs and turned I wasn't prepared for a mop-haired blonde, about five-one in a brown dress that barely covered the V where her legs joined together, and who wore a saucy, go to hell grin, and who dragged a long, suede coat, and who wanted to know if I, for Christ sake, was Philip St. Ives.

"I'm St. Ives."

She frowned at a slip of paper she held. "Where the hell are the other two, Mr. Costly and Mr. Expensive?" She thrust the paper at me. "That's what it says, Jack; I didn't make it up."

I wondered if Coors had chuckled over his little joke.

"They couldn't come," I said. "Instead, I brought Mr. Wisdom, who's the solid-looking gentleman on your left, and Mr. Knight, the handsome devil your right."

She grinned and stuck out her small hand and gave me a firm grip and then did the same thing to Wisdom and Knight. "I'm Arrie Tonzi," she said, "and I'm your official embassy escort and if you don't like girls, then you'll have to see somebody about it tomorrow, because you're stuck with me this afternoon."

"I think you're beautiful, Miss Tonzi," Wisdom said and smiled mournfully.

"I think the State Department has been most thoughtful," Knight said, giving her his best smile.

"You're right," she said to me, "he is goddamned handsome."

"He's an actor feller," I said. "Sneaky."

"Hey! I know *you!*" she said to Knight.

"I'd rather have money than fame," Wisdom said to no one in particular.

She put her face up close to Knight's and stared at it. Then she snapped her fingers with a loud pop. In his face. "You did the lonesome fireman in all those deodorant commercials about two years ago."

"Yes," Knight said. "We'd fallen upon hard times."

"If it weren't for his residuals, he'd be a pauper," Wisdom told the girl. "I, on the other hand, am rich beyond your wildest dreams and am I not fair of countenance?"

"Who're you," she said, "Wisdom or Knight? I'm no good at names."

"I'm Wisdom," he said. "Knight's the prettied-up, married one over there."

"Did your wife come?" she said to Knight.

"She couldn't make it."

"Good," she said and turned to me, dragging her long coat over the floor. "What are you, St. Ives, the tour leader?"

"Something like that."

"You do this for a living?"

"What?"

"Ransom ambassadors."

"It's my first ambasador," I said. "I started out West, first ransoming sheep, then worked up to horses, and finally to people. But this is my first ambassador and I hope you don't mind if I'm just a little nervous."

She widened her stance, put her fists on her hips, and looked up at me. "I would say you're putting me on, but I can't stand the phrase. You are bullshitting me, aren't you?"

Wisdom sidled up behind her and whispered hoarsely into her ear. "Look at his pallor, doll. The guy's no more'n a week out of Dannemora."

"Who *is* he?" she demanded of me.

"Mr. Wisdom provides our comic relief," I said seriously. "He's young and brash and fun loving. Mr. Knight, a wiser, older head, will shortly pull out a briar pipe and suck on it to demonstrate his sadly gentle disapproval of Mr. Wisdom's exuberance. I serve as the levelheaded balance, equally tol-

68

erant of youth's foolish foibles and middle-age's dull despair."

"I think you're also the chief bullshitter," she said.

Knight gestured with his pipe and leered at her. "You holding, baby?"

"Jesus," she said. "One actor and two nuts. I'm attached to the press attaché and he assigned me to stick with you and guide you around and see that you don't get lost and order your meals and wipe your noses and buy presents for your wives."

"The actor there's the only one who's married, ma'am," Wisdom said. "I'm a single man myself and Mr. St. Ives here's become sort of a rakehell since his divorce."

"Oh, Jesus," she said. "I wish I were Catholic so I could pray." She looked up at me. "I'm also your translator if any of you ever shut up long enough to need one."

"Okay," I said. "What's our hotel?"

"I booked you in at the Metropol," she said.

"*Je Metropol hotel jedan dobar hotel?*" Wisdom asked her quickly.

She turned on him. "I thought none of you spoke the language."

Wisdom smiled and patted her rounded butt. "Don't worry, love," he said, winking. "It's the only phrase I know."

"You do speak it, Arrie?" I said.

"My father was a Hungarian who got us out in fifty-six," she said. "My mother's a Yugoslav. A Serb. We speak everything. We have to."

"How long have you been with the State Department?" Knight asked her.

"Four years," she said. "Hell, it's almost five now. I was in Prague for two and I've been here nearly two. Have you got all of your luggage or have you lost half of it?"

"We didn't bring much since we're not staying long."

"The car's outside. When do you want to start tomorrow, early?"

"What's early?"

"Eight—eight thirty."

"It's the middle of the goddamned night," the actor stated and then looked around for someone to contradict him. Nobody did.

"Nine," she said. "They speak English at the Metropol so you can manage breakfast by yourselves. The only thing I have you scheduled for in the morning is the Ministry of Interior. You're to meet a Mr. Bartak there at eleven."

"What's it about?"

"I thought you knew," she said, "I don't. They haven't told me a goddamned thing because everybody's got their bowels in an uproar about old grab-ass being kidnapped."

"Still at it, huh?" I said.

"He never misses a chance and the younger the better."

"All right," I said. "We see Mr. Bartak and then what?"

"Then lunch. After that, you go calling on a Nobel poet. Anton Pernik."

"Does he speak English?"

"I don't know if he does, but his granddaughter does. If you want me to translate for you, I will."

I said, "We'll see," and then we pushed through the entrance to the airport and waited for the black embassy four-door-Ford sedan which seems the standard U.S. conveyance for those who are greeted at foreign airports by the assistant to the press attaché. If you rank slightly higher up the protocol scale, you get a big new Mercury, also black.

It was my first trip to Belgrade so I couldn't compare it to what it had looked like before the Germans flattened it in

70

1941, or what it had looked like five or ten years ago when the building boom was on, or even 1500 years ago when the Huns sacked and razed it or when the Crusaders wandered through it in the eleventh century or when it was captured by the Turks in 1521. But on the twelve-mile trip into the city it looked new and fairly clean with lots of glass and concrete apartment buildings. In fact, it looked very much like Bonn and Barcelona and Birmingham (either England or Alabama) and I wished that it didn't, but most cities look very much alike today.

Arrie Tonzi sat up front with the embassy driver and pointed out a few sights, but she really didn't have her heart in it. When we pulled up at the Metropol, I asked her to join us in a drink, but she shook her head no and said that she had to get back to the embassy.

"Change your mind about the drink," Wisdom urged.

She smiled and shook her head. "Some other time," she said.

"It is *Miss* Tonzi, isn't it?" he said.

"Miss Tonzi, twenty-six, a maiden lady of uncertain prospects."

"If only you'd forget your pride and let me help you!" Wisdom said or cried, I guess, with an appropriate gesture.

"He is sort of cute, if a little pudgy," she said to Knight.

Knight put his hands on her shoulders and stared down at her. "There's something wrong with his glands, but here in Belgrade there's a doctor who may be able to help. Still, over the years there have been many doctors, and if this treatment fails, well—"

"Jesus," she said to me. "Does it go on like this all the time?"

"Only when they've got an audience."

"You can check in and get up to your rooms by yourselves, can't you?"

"I think we can manage."

"It's going to be fun, I can tell."

"Let's hope so," I said.

Arrie Tonzi had a pretty little face with a mouth that kept going in and out of an uncertain smile, eyes that were too large one moment and squinted up into smiling arcs the next, a fair complexion that probably tanned well in summer, and a good enough figure which you could see most of if you peeped, and she didn't seem to care much if you did. I suppose she was one of the first volunteers in the no-bra movement. She stood now in what seemed to be her favorite stance, her legs planted a little widely apart, her fists on her hips, trying to make her 102 or 103 pounds look tough and aggressive and not missing the desired effect by more than a couple of miles. She wanted to say something and she wasn't quite sure how she should say it but she was damned sure going to say it anyhow.

"Is what you're going to do going to be dangerous? I mean getting the ambasador back?"

"No," I said. "I don't think so. If it were going to be dangerous, they probably would have sent somebody else."

"Well—" She stopped and then started over again. "Well, I mean, if it *is* going to be dangerous and you need some help, well, what I mean is you can—oh, hell, I know it sounds corny, but goddamn it, St. Ives, you can call on me."

"Thanks, Arrie. I appreciate that. I really do."

She looked at me carefully. "Like shit you do," she said and turned and walked back to the embassy car.

We made it up to our rooms without any trouble and I was lying down, testing the bed, when the phone rang. There was no one I wanted to talk to, not Knight or Wisdom or Arrie Tonzi or Artur Bjelo or Anton Pernik or Amfred Killingsworth, especially not Amfred Killingsworth, but I picked up the phone on its third double ring and answered it anyway.

"Mr. St. Ives?" It was a man's voice, accented, a little muffled.

"Yes," I said.

"Jovan Tavro here."

"All right," I said. "You name it, where and when?"

"Good," he said. "You are quick—no nonsense. I like that."

"Fine," I said. "Name it."

"The Café Nemoguće," he said. "It's near the Central Station. Nemoguće means 'impossible' in English. That is funny, is it not?" and he laughed harshly to let me know that he at least thought so.

"Very," I said. "What time?"

"Ten o'clock."

"Any recognition?"

"Order some *plejescavitsa*," he said. "An American eating *plejescavitsa* should be recognizable enough."

"I can't even pronounce it," I said, but he had already hung up.

CHAPTER 9

I took a 1939 Plymouth taxi to the Central Station and walked from there. With sign language, a smattering of German, and a few phrases of French, I was directed north along Gavrila Principa past Kamenica Street and then left on a street that dead-ended into a triangular-shaped park that seemed to be about three blocks from the Sava River.

The wind blew in from the river, cold and wet. There was hardly any traffic and the pedestrians looked as if they were in a hurry to get home to a glass of something warm. The Café Nemoguće had been allotted an impossibly narrow slice of the ground floor of a new office building, grudgingly it seemed, and on fair days there was room on the sidewalk to set out the half-dozen tables and their chairs which were now neatly stacked near the entrance. I suppose the café got its name from its narrow width, which was no more than nine feet, but inside it seemed to run back forever.

I chose a table near the door and the newspaper rack. The

café was neither crowded nor empty and most of the customers seemed deeply involved in their conversation which they carried on in voices loud enough for me to overhear or perhaps even join if I could have spoken the language.

I've never tried to pass for a native in any European country, not even in London where, if you keep your mouth shut, you might have a fifty-fifty chance. But in the rest of Europe, unless you've lived there long enough to get a haircut and buy some clothes off the peg, you might as well have "Donated by U.S.A." stamped right across your forehead. It's in the walk maybe, or the shape of the butt, or perhaps the facial expression, but almost anyone can spot Americans in Europe, even if they keep their mouths shut and even if they're alone, although neither happens very often.

So it was no surprise when the waiter welcomed me in English to his country, city, neighborhood, and café and then asked in German how things were going back in the States and how long I'd been in Yugoslavia and then switched to Serbo-Croatian to ask what I wanted to eat (at least he kept pointing at the menu) and then nodded his melancholy agreement when I told him that I'd try the *plejescavitsa*.

"*Und ein Schnapps, ja?*" he said, back in German again, and I agreed that ein Schnapps was just what I needed so he brought me a large thimbleful of *slivovica* which is a plum brandy of about 140 proof whose warming qualities were so reassuring that I promptly called for another round.

The *plejescavitsa* turned out to be a dozen balls of well-seasoned ground meat—beef, veal and pork, I think—with some odd bits of lamb and sweet pepper that had been spitted and grilled. It was quite good, as was the salad that came with it, and the combined culinary success seemed to call for another *slivovica*. I was halfway through it when the man with the face like an unhappy carp sat down at my table. I smiled and nodded at him and started to ask if he'd care for a drink, but before I could speak, he said, "We can talk here as well as any place. I'm Tavro."

"You care for anything?" I said.

"Coffee."

I ordered two coffees from the waiter who nodded familiarly at Tavro as if he were a regular customer. The coffee was a Turkish legacy, sweet and thick and black, and Tavro sipped his noisily.

"You know anyone called Bjelo who looks something like me but who's about ten years younger?"

"No," Tavro said. "Why do you ask?"

"I keep running into him. I thought he might be interested in you."

Tavro wagged his thick head from side to side. "Nobody has much official interest in me now except for the pair that keeps me under surveillance. But since I make it a point to be here every night, they no longer come inside but sleep in their car instead."

"Have you tried this before?" I said.

"To leave? No. I've had no reason to."

"But you have one now?"

Tavro was somewhere in his late fifties, not tall but big-boned and wide, except for his shoulders which seemed curiously narrow until I realized that his thick neck made them appear that way. The neck was corded with heavy muscles and tendons that gave it a fluted appearance, something like a sturdy Doric column. His head was not much wider than his neck, dished in shape, and it turned carefully and slowly as if it were kept up there with the aid of a brace. It was a peculiarly Slavic face with high cheekbones that

76

planed out from the curved nose which beaked toward the wide, petty mouth. It was a hard, mean, ugly face and I wondered how much of it Tavro was responsible for.

"Is your task to interrogate me, Mr. St. Ives, or to help me get across the border?"

"When I think I need to ask questions, I will, so I'll ask another one right now. Which border? You've got seven of them."

"Not the Albanian, of course," he said.

"No."

"And I despise Hungarians, which eliminates that. The Greeks are still impossible, the Rumanians inhospitable, and I never did trust a Bulgar, so that leaves either Italy or Austria, doesn't it?"

"Either one?"

"Either one."

"All right," I said.

"When?" he said.

"I don't know."

"How?"

"I don't know that either."

Tavro folded his big-knuckled hands on the table. The hair on their backs was black and white and matched the thick, shortcropped covering on his head. His eyebrows, however, were still a fierce, bristly black and the pale blue eyes that glared out at me from beneath them shone not with tears, but with a contempt so intense that it glistened.

"Do you work for your government, Mr. St. Ives?"

"No."

"You are an entrepreneur, a free agent of sorts?"

"Of sorts."

"Then there is none that I can complain to?"

"None I can think of, unless you want to try the ambassador, but I understand he's pretty busy right now."

"That fool."

"You tried him, didn't you?"

"It was a mistake. He offered much in exchange for what I gave him, but returned nothing."

"He's like that," I said.

"Do you know him?"

"I know him."

"Do you think there is a chance that his kidnappers might kill him?"

"I don't know."

"It would be convenient, if they did."

"Convenient for whom?" I said.

He shrugged. "For mankind, let's say."

I nodded. "When I come up with a scheme to get you out, how do I get in touch?"

"Thank you for saying when and not if," Tavro said and took a small notebook from his dark, boxlike coat, wrote something down, tore out a page, and handed it to me. There was an address and a name; the name was Bill Jones.

"Bill Jones?" I said.

He nodded, smiling and chuckling nastily, much as he had done over the phone when he found the name of the café amusing. "He is a countryman of yours and an old friend of mine. We were together during the war. Afterwards, because of a girl, my friend Bill Jones came back and now here he lives." He pronounced Jones as if it began with a *Y*, but that's what happens to the *J* in Yugoslavia.

"What's he do?" I said.

Tavro shrugged. "He has done what any man must do to earn his living. He has driven a lorry and laid bricks and car-

78

pentered and dug ditches and repaired machinery. He is a man who can use his hands but who has never worked in a factory. And to my knowledge he has never worked long at anything, but still he has raised a family."

"What's he do when he's not working?" I said.

"He fishes and when he's not fishing, he hunts. And when he's doing neither, he sits in the café and drinks his brandy and reads his newspaper and gossips with the rest. He is not an intellectual, Mr. St. Ives. He is just a man who fought well during the war, liked the country in which he fought, and who returned to live and work in it. And if he did not work too hard or make too great a contribution, what does that matter?"

"Not much," I said.

"Do you find it strange that an American would do this?"

"I'd find it strange if many did it, but not one."

"He has no politics. If you wish to get a message to me, leave it with him."

"It'll probably be a few days," I said.

"It must be no longer than that."

"You're in a hurry?"

Tavro produced a cigarette and carefully turned it in his big fingers before lighting it. "I assume that you know who I was at one time and what post I held?"

I nodded. "Confidential assistant to the head of your secret police. I don't remember what they call it."

"They call it the UDBA," he said. "I was accused, whether justly or unjustly is of no matter now, along with Vice-President Rankovic and removed from my post. For the past several years I have done little. I have read a great deal, something I never had time for before, and I have raised some fine flowers—do you care for flowers, Mr. St. Ives, for roses, especially?"

"Roses are fine," I said.

"I have been exceptionally fortunate with mine. But to continue, I have lived these past few years, except for the surveillance which is now only cursory, much as a man in exile might live. I have few friends, none of them in government. My family is scattered, my wife is dead. So I thought that I had been forgotten, as a deposed politician should be. I was mistaken."

"How?"

"There are those who want the information I have. At first they tried to persuade me. I refused. Then they threatened me and—" He spread his hands. "I believed them."

"So you went to see Killingsworth," I said.

"Yes. A fatuous man, but still shrewd enough not to offer me help unless I first gave him the information—one hundred and two pages of it."

"And then he got kidnapped," I said.

"Yes," Tavro said, nodding a little cynically. "Kidnapped. Convenient wasn't it?"

"I wouldn't know," I said. "How long do you think you have?"

"Before what?"

"Before whoever wants you to give them that information carries out their threat—whatever it is."

"The threat, Mr. St. Ives, is that they will kill me. I have every reason to believe them."

I nodded. "All right. How long do you have?"

He shrugged. "Five days, possibly six." He gestured almost apologetically. "There is no set deadline."

"That's still cutting it thin," I said.

"Yes, Mr. St. Ives, it is. You have only a few hours to come up with a successful plan. However, there is one consolation."

"What?"

He rose, leaned toward me over the table, and smiled unpleasantly. It may have been the only way he could smile. "If the plan that you devise in these next few days and hours fails," he said, "it is entirely possible that you will have several years of solitude to determine why it did. *Laku noc.*"

CHAPTER **10**

At eight the next morning there was a call from Arrie Tonzi who said that she was downstairs with a mumbled name who was the embassy's press or public affairs attaché and that they were on their way up. I immediately ordered coffee and then went into the bathroom and by the time I came out they were knocking at the door.

"You're early, aren't you?" I said as she came in wearing a blue dress whose skirt was even shorter than the one she'd worn the day before. I noticed that she still dragged the long suede coat.

"Not really," she said, picking out a chair and crossing her legs before she sank into it. "The normal Yugoslav workday is seven till two. Philip St. Ives, Gordon Lehmann. Gordon's the public affairs attaché."

I shook hands with a middling-tall man in his late twenties whose shy, pleasant face looked far too honest for him ever to do well in public relations. "I've got fifty reporters in town yelling for a statement and I haven't got anything to tell them," he said. "All we can get out of Washington is to check with you."

"They've got the ransom demand, haven't they?" I said.

"They've already milked that dry. They want to talk to the go-between."

"Can't they get something out of Anton Pernik?"

"He won't talk to them. Or at least that's what the four government cops who're guarding his apartment say."

"Have they issued any statement?"

"The government?"

I nodded and Lehmann said, "Only a new version about how for humanitarian reasons and to maintain the excellent relations that they enjoy with the U.S. government they will release Pernik from protective custody et cetera and so on."

"You'd better throw them a fish."

"How?" he said.

I turned to Arrie Tonzi. "What time's my appointment with the guy at the Ministry of Interior?"

"With Bartak? At eleven."

I looked at Lehmann. "Why don't you set up a press conference for me here at the hotel at half past noon?"

"You really want to talk to them?" he said and I was sure then that his honesty would forever bar him from the big time which might be too bad for the country, if not for him.

"No," I said, "I don't want to talk to them, but I'll have to eventually and I'd rather choose the time than have a couple of them pop up from behind the hedgerow just as I'm handing Pernik over for the ambassador."

He nodded and then asked, "Have you heard from the kidnappers?"

"We'd also better get the rules straight," I said. "If I hear from the kidnappers, I may or may not decide to tell you about it. It depends entirely on what kind of proposal they make. This is going to be a tricky exchange because it involves not only three persons, but also a million dollars. When I accepted this assignment in Washington, I was assured that I would be in full charge. If I still am, then I'll have to run it my way."

It was a pompous little speech full of lies and distortions, with only a kernel or two of truth, and I was sorry that I had to feed it to Lehmann who seemed like a decent enough person, the kind who should be teaching journalism at some state university, but it contained a lot of what I was going to give the press so I had to see how well it went down. It went down so well that I thought Lehmann might lick his lips for more.

He had a long, slender head that he nodded at me now, almost eagerly, as if trying to show how anxious he was to cooperate. "We've been told to give you what you need," he said, "but if you could talk to the press and explain why the negotiations have to be kept under wraps, it would certainly be a relief to me."

"Fine, then set it up for twelve thirty and I'll give them what I can."

"I'll get right on it."

"There's another thing," I told him and after he asked what, I said, "When the kidnappers sent their original ransom demand, how'd they do it?"

"It was a phone call to the embassy."

"Not to Killingsworth's wife?"

"No, she's been pretty much kept out of it."

"Good."

84

"Is that what you're expecting, a phone call?" Lehmann asked.

"I don't care what it is as long as I hear from them."

"When do you think that'll be?"

"I don't know."

"Have you set any deadline?"

"Yes."

"When is it?"

I smiled at him. "It's when I start worrying because I haven't heard from them."

After calling Knight and asking him and Wisdom to monitor the press conference, I let Arrie Tonzi watch me eat a skimpy breakfast in the hotel dining room while she had some more coffee. The Yugoslavs, I found, aren't at all keen about breakfast.

"You're different this morning," she said.

"How?"

"You seem to know what you're doing."

"You mean I didn't yesterday?"

She reached over and took one of my cigarettes and lit it before I thought to do anything about it. "All you had yesterday were a lot of smart-ass cracks that weren't as funny as they could have been."

"It was a long flight," I said.

"See?"

"See what?"

"You're starting that funny-funny stuff again. You were different when you were handling Lehmann. You're good at it, aren't you?"

"At what?"

"At handling nice guys like Lehmann so they don't know that they're being handled."

"It's all part of the job."

"Can I sit in when you talk to Bartak?"

"Do you want to?"

"Yes."

"Why?"

"I want to see how you handle someone who's not so nice. From what I hear, Bartak's a real prick."

We drew the same driver and as far as I could tell the same Ford as the day before. Arrie Tonzi sat in back with me and pointed out the sights as we drove down the wide Bulevar Revolucije which I shrewdly translated into Boulevard of the Revolution without too much difficulty.

"That's the main post office," Arrie said and I gave it a dutiful glance. "And on your right for the next block or so is what they used to call the Parliament, but which is now known as the Federal Assembly."

"A little architectural influence from the Hapsburgs, I'd say."

She nodded. "If they didn't have to put up with the Austrians, it was the Hungarians or the Venetians, and as if that weren't bad enough, then came the Germans and way before that, the Turks and the Romans, and the Huns. There's always been somebody tromping through Yugoslavia and telling them how to live. I don't blame Tito for telling the Russians to bug off."

"It wasn't quite like that," I said.

"I like to think it was." She poked me in the arm. "Look to your left, across the park, and you can see the Royal Palace. The park used to be the Royal Gardens but they just call it the park now."

I looked and decided that it was more Viennese whipped cream. I remember that King Peter had lived there just before the war and I wondered where he lived now and if he really had any hope of living in the Palace again.

We turned left on Brankova Prizrenska and approached a bridge that crossed the Sava River. "Over there is Novi Beograd, or New Belgrade," Arrie said. "Before the war, it was nothing but swamp, but now it's got skyscrapers and museums and blocks of flats and lots of culture."

"I don't mind swamps," I said.

"That tall thing is the Communist Presidium and Conference headquarters. Twenty-six stories high. The Presidium runs things but it's supervised by the annual Conference."

"It's a nice building," I said. "This is on the way to the airport, isn't it?"

"Yes," she said. "I could have pointed it all out to you yesterday, but you didn't seem too interested."

"That's probably because they're all beginning to look alike," I said.

"What?"

"Cities and towns. The European towns that were destroyed by the war didn't just lose some buildings, they lost the flavor that made Zagreb different from Aachen, if you like to alphabetize things. When they design buildings now, they avoid the baroque and the rococo because it's expensive and it's not really needed and that's fine. But they also avoid giving buildings any distinctive character of their own and so an office building in Moscow looks pretty much like an office building in Manhattan."

"And you don't like that?"

"Not much."

"What do you want?"

"Hell, I don't know. A little Tabasco in the plans, I guess. Even some whimsy. What's wrong with a dash of fey in the design for the Ministry for Cultural Affairs as long as it lets in the light and keeps out the weather?"

"What do you think of that one?" she asked. "Got enough fey in it for you?"

It was a sweeping, graceful building which rose just the other side of the bridge.

"What is it?" I asked.

"The Museum of Modern Art," she said. "What do you think?"

"I like it."

"You won't like the Ministry of Interior," she said. "No Tabasco."

She was right. It was a plain, ugly building, seven stories high and perhaps six years old, that was built conveniently close to the Presidium skyscraper. Inside there was the usual fuss about whom we wanted to see and where we wanted to go and while one of the uniformed guards was on the telephone, I examined a mural done in harsh yellows and reds and blues and unhappy browns that tried to portray the accomplishments of one of Tito's five-year plans. I assumed that the plan had been more successful than the mural, but then I've seldom liked murals.

I never did get a satisfactory translation for Slobodan Bartak's title (he was either deputy assistant minister or deputy to the assistant minister), but from the size of his office I could tell that he was a comer and from the ambition on his youthful face, I expected him to go a far way.

He was still in his early thirties, but when Arrie Tonzi displayed an unconsciously generous portion of both crotch and thigh as she sat down, it drew only a quick glance from Bartak and if there were any reaction other than a flicker of prudish disapproval, I failed to detect it.

Bartak hadn't risen when we were ushered in, and we hadn't shaken hands, and he hadn't done much of anything other than to nod that he was aware of our existence, if not thrilled by it, and that if we liked, we could sit down. There were two files on his desk, a thin green one and a fat blue one. He flipped through the fat blue one for a while and when he got tired of that he opened the thin green one and pressed its spine down so that it would lie flat on his desk. On the page that he turned to there was a picture, about three by five inches, and even upside down, I didn't think it did me justice.

He looked up from the photo at me and then back at the photo again. "This is your first visit to our country, Mr. St. Ives." It was no question so I made no answer. "I hope you enjoy your stay, what little there will be of it."

"I hope so, too," I said because he seemed to be waiting for something—maybe to decide whether he liked the tone of my voice.

He shifted his glance to Arrie Tonzi and then back again to me. "Will Miss Tonzi serve as your translator throughout the negotiations?" he said.

"I don't know yet. I don't even know if a translator will be required."

"It may be too much to hope that our criminals are bilingual." I smiled at that, assuming it was a joke.

"We are extremely interested in capturing the kidnappers." He paused. "Once the ambassador is safe, of course."

I nodded and wondered how long it would take him to get

around to it. It had once taken a Chicago detective bureau lieutenant forty-six minutes, but the detective had been so thick-witted that it took him a quarter of an hour to order breakfast. I'd timed him.

In criminal negotiations that make use of a go-between, it is to be expected that the law will offer him a proposal while the crook will make him a proposition. The proposition will fatten the go-between's wallet as well as the crook's while the proposal will benefit only the law, unless the go-between is unusual in his need of warm praise from such persons as assistant district attorneys, police precinct captains, and county sheriffs. But both underworld proposition and civic proposal are based on some variance of the double cross and I was interested in what Bartak's version would be. He got right to it.

"It has occurred to me, Mr. St. Ives, that with a little skillful planning and some cooperation from you, it might be possible to apprehend the kidnappers without endangering the ambassador. Have you given this any thought?"

"None," I said.

"My country regards kidnapping as a most reprehensible crime."

"Most countries do."

"If the kidnappers were caught and brought to swift justice, it would serve as a strong deterrent to any similar attempts in the future."

"I might argue that," I said, "but I wouldn't argue that whoever caught them would increase his chances for promotion."

Bartak closed the thin green folder carefully. He locked his hands together and rested them on top of it. He frowned to show that he was displeased with my remark. He then

90

pulled his chin back toward his Adam's apple to indicate that despite his displeasure he was going to make his proposal anyway. I waited.

"For many reasons, Mr. St. Ives, not the least of them being the simple, humanitarian ones, we have offered our full cooperation in securing the release of your ambassador. At the same time we cannot afford to appear indifferent toward the perpetration of the crime. Our chief interest lies in the safe return of Mr. Killingsworth. But we are vitally concerned with punishing the kidnappers. We believe that we have a plan which, with only a small measure of cooperation from you, will enable us to do both. It will also serve—"

I decided to cut him short. "If you have such a plan, Mr. Bartak, I'm sure it's a good one, but I don't want to hear it."

He had a young face, one not yet old enough to conceal surprise, especially at something unpleasant, and for a moment he looked like a four-year-old who's just learned the hard way that old Ruff can bite.

The frown returned to his sloping forehead, his stubby nose wrinkled as if it smelled gas, and his wide, thick mouth screwed itself up into something that lay between a pout and a snarl. The calm was gone from his voice, too, and when he spoke the words came tumbling out over each other as if in frantic haste to leave so that they could jump up and down on me.

"I must regard your remark as an insult directed at my government and myself!" he said, almost sputtering. "Your discourtesy endangers all chances for cooperation and, furthermore, it could endanger the life of your ambassador. This is no simple matter, Mr. St. Ives. I must point out that your refusal to cooperate with us in so important an undertaking may well cause my government to review its arrangements with the United States in other—"

I decided to break in again before I started World War III. "I'm deeply sorry if you interpreted my refusal to listen to your proposal as an insult, Mr. Bartak. It wasn't meant to be and I apologize if it created such a misunderstanding. However, you must understand that as the private intermediary in this transaction I have certain obligations to the kidnappers as well as to the victim."

I was going to continue but he interrupted, still excited. "You admit your obligation to criminals!" It seemed like a good point and he grabbed it and would have been off down the sidelines unless I pushed him out of bounds.

"Ambassador Killingsworth's life, Mr. Bartak, may well depend on whether I fulfill my obligations to the criminals." That got his attention, so I gave him the rest of it. "They didn't hesitate to kidnap him. They won't hesitate to kill the only witness to their crime if they suspect even the slightest trickery. So yes, you might say I have an obligation to the kidnappers and that obligation is to keep them happy and content."

Bartak shook his head. He was a stubborn one. "The plan that you so rudely rejected, even before you knew its content, was designed with Mr. Killingsworth's safety foremost in mind. We have cooperated fully with your government in this entire matter, even to the point of releasing Anton Pernik. I assure you that we would not advance a plan that would endanger the life of the ambassador."

"No, I'm sure you wouldn't," I said. "But if I were a party to it, and something did happen, then it would be my responsibility. I won't take that chance, not only because I'm concerned with Ambassador Killingsworth's safety, but because I'm also very much concerned with mine."

Telling them that you are a coward is always the easiest way out. They can understand that whether they are a Chicago detective bureau lieutenant or a high official in the Ministry of Interior. It also makes them feel superior. It made Bartak feel that way and he leaped at the chance to show me just how much.

"There is the distinct possibility, Mr. St. Ives, that the plan I spoke of does not depend entirely upon your cooperation."

"I didn't think that it would," I said, "but I still don't want to know what it is. This way I go into negotiations with what the lawyers call clean hands. If something goes wrong with your plan, neither you nor the kidnappers can blame me, because I know nothing about it. Is that satisfactory?"

Bartak thought about it for a moment. To help him do it, he drummed his fingers on the surface of his nicely polished desk. "Yes," he said finally. "We have not entirely lost the element of surprise because you are certainly in no position to warn the kidnappers."

"You're right," I said. "I'm not."

He nodded his head, well satisfied with himself and with the way the morning had gone, and for all I knew, with his prospects for rapid advancement.

"Can I be of any further service to you, Mr. St. Ives?"

"I need the papers that will allow Anton Pernik and his granddaughter to leave Yugoslavia."

"Of course," he said and drew the fat blue file toward him, opened it, and took out a thick brown envelope. Before handing it to me, he said, "You understand, of course, that these papers are only exit permits. They are not passports. Once Pernik and his granddaughter have crossed its border, Yugoslavia is no longer responsible for their safety and well-being. They forfeit their rights to citizenships."

"I understand," I said and accepted the envelope.

Bartak rose. He was shorter than I'd thought, not more than five-foot-two or three. It may have been why he hadn't risen when we came in. Or it may have been that his height didn't concern him at all, but I doubted that, preferring to believe that he was the Ministry's resident authority on Napoleon.

"I hope you also understand something else, Mr. St. Ives," he said.

"What?"

"I hope you understand that while our concern for the safety of Ambassador Killingsworth is tremendously grave, that same degree of concern cannot be extended to Anton Pernik and his granddaughter." I was about to tell him that I understood that fully, but he hurried on. Smoothly. "Or, for that matter, to you."

CHAPTER **11**

It was my second press conference within five days and it was pointless to argue about which of them had been the better farce. The one about the rats in New York probably had contained more substance while the one in Belgrade seemed to have more style, perhaps because of the international press corps. There weren't three paragraphs of hard news in either of them.

But the one at the Metropol hotel did serve to help establish my bona fides as a private citizen who was what he said he was: an industrious, hardworking go-between and not what the press wished that I was: a tool—unwitting or otherwise—of the CIA or the State Department or something equally flamboyant.

They asked me some questions and I told them some lies when I had to and the truth when there was no point in lying. We traded a few smart remarks and, upon request, I gave them a couple of brief, overly lurid accounts of two other kidnappings that I'd been called in on. The Italians like those. Or perhaps they just liked Arrie Tonzi's translation which she rendered in a melodramatic tone accompanied by appropriate gestures.

"We'll take care of the cost of the meeting room," Gordon Lehmann said when the conference was over. It was something that he thought I might be worrying about. It wasn't but I thanked him anyway and asked him to join us for lunch. He shook his head and said that he should get back to the embassy.

"What's that address?" I said.

"Kneza Milosa fifty," he said and spelled it for me. "The phone's 645-655. Extension seventeen."

While I was writing it down on the back of my airline ticket he said, "Were you ever in PR, Phil?"

I told him no, that I'd never had the pleasure, that I'd always worked for newspapers, and mentioned the name of the one that I'd worked for in New York and he said he remembered my column and then asked, "Do you think it would be helpful if I got some actual newspaper experience? I came right to State from school."

It would take more than that, I thought, but said, "I don't think it's really necessary, Gordon." And then, because he very much seemed to need something more, I added, "You're doing a hell of a fine job here." It was a lie, but since I had been lying all morning, to almost anyone who would listen, one more couldn't hurt anything and it might even keep him from brooding the rest of the afternoon away.

They really should try as hard to keep sensitive people out of public relations as they do to keep embezzlers out of banks. But my line or two of praise was all that Lehmann's ego needed, at least till suppertime, and he headed happily back to the embassy to compose a brilliant aide-mémoire or two on the conference.

At my elbow, Arrie Tonzi said, "You're full of nifties, aren't you?"

"Why?"

"In just one morning I get to watch you put the slam on Bartak, handle the press conference like you'd scripted it, and then find time to administer to the tortured sensibilities of our press attaché, poor wretch."

"He's all right," I said.

"He's miserable and you know it. That's why you spread the word balm on. Either you're schizy, St. Ives, or beneath that grim exterior beats a bleeding heart."

"Don't count on it," I said. "Let's eat."

We were joined at lunch by Wisdom and Knight who had been sitting at the rear of the press conference. When I asked what they thought of it, Wisdom said that it had been highly informative, but my jokes were old. Knight said he had found it entertaining and amusing, but noticed that I lacked stage presence and offered to teach me a few simple but useful gestures.

"Anything else?" I said.

"What's on for later, after our naps?" Wisdom asked.

"We go calling on the Nobel poet and his granddaughter."

"Have you got anything to tell them yet," Knight asked, "such as how or when or where?"

"Not yet."

"This is just a get-acquainted session?" Wisdom said.

"That's right."

"What if they don't like me?"

"Eat your caviar," I said. "It's fresh from the Danube."

It took Arrie Tonzi five phone calls to get all the permissions that were needed for us to make an appointment with Anton Pernik.

"He doesn't have a phone," she said when she came back from making the last call, "but someone in Bartak's office will send him a telegram. The appointment's for four o'clock. You want me to go along?"

"I think so," I said, "if it's convenient for you."

"I'd like to meet him."

At fifteen minutes to four we were heading south on Marshal Tito Avenue which seemed to be about twice as wide as Pennsylvania Avenue but handled less than a tenth as much traffic. We followed the avenue for a mile or so and then turned left. After that I was lost. The driver made three or four more turns, moving deeper into what seemed to be a district devoted to six- and seven-storied flats that wore their depressing sameness like shabby uniforms.

We pulled up before one that seemed no different from the scores of others we had passed except for the two men in dark suits who lounged inside the entrance and who might as well have carried signs advertising that they were plainclothes cops.

Arrie had a chat with them and showed them her credentials and then introduced us and they smiled and spoke politely, but insisted on looking at our passports. One of them accompanied us into the building and up two flights of stairs where he greeted two more plainclothesmen, who were just as friendly, but who didn't insist on examining our passports. We followed the cop who'd escorted us from below down the hall. He knocked on an apartment door politely. While we waited we smiled at each other as strangers do whose language difference bars them from talking about the weather which was a little warmer than it had been the day before.

When the door opened I completely understood why Amfred Killingsworth had told the U.S. Department of State to go to hell. Although beauty and loveliness are totally inadequate words, she had the kind that could make kings abdicate, presidents abscond, and prime ministers turn to treason.

There was the wildness of the Balkans about her, and the sadness too, and they blended into an almost impossible loveliness that promised to share some wickedly delightful secret. The sea was in her eyes, the somber chill, gray-blue of the winter Adriatic. But if you looked more deeply there was also the laughing promise of next summer's golden warmth. Her hair, long, thick, black, and begging for a touch, fell almost to her waist. It carelessly framed a pale oval face that had two eyes, a nose, a mouth, and a chin, and if you had lived an absolutely blameless, sinless life, the reward of just one long close look at that perfect symmetry would have made it worth all the bother.

Although the plainclothes guard must have seen her every day, he was still struck dumb. First to recover was Wisdom who swallowed and said, "My name's Park Tyler Wisdom and I've come to take you away from all this."

She looked at Park and smiled, which made her look only more lovely than before. "You are not Mr. St. Ives?" she said.

"I am," I said. "I'm St. Ives. I'm Philip St. Ives." I probably would have gone on babbling my name for the rest of the day if Knight's elbow hadn't found my kidney. I recovered enough to introduce him and Arrie Tonzi who whispered to me, "She's simply stunning."

"I hadn't noticed," I said.

"I am Gordana Panić," she said. "My grandfather is expecting you. Please do come in."

We followed her down a short entry hall that led to a sitting room that was furnished with dark, solid pieces that looked as if they were accustomed to far more space. The walls contained framed photographs of men alone and in groups and from the way they combed their hair and the style of their collars, I assumed that most of them had been dead for some time.

Gordana Panić saw to it that each of us was seated comfortably. She continued to stand by a large, leather-covered chair that was near a door. She stood with unconscious, perfect poise, her long slender hands clasped loosely in front of her. The dress she wore was something blue and white, I think. I remember that it was neither too close nor too loose nor too long nor too short and that it revealed the outlines of her soft breasts and slender waist and remarkable hips and thighs that tapered into long, bare, perfectly formed legs. I couldn't tell about her feet because she wore shoes, ugly black ones, and I decided to buy her new ones, probably in Paris, even if I had to kill Park Tyler Wisdom III to do it.

When the old man came into the room, she helped him into the big, leather-covered chair. "This is my grandfather, Anton Pernik," she said. "If you speak slowly and loudly, he can understand you." She bent down and said something in Serbo-Croatian to the old man and he shook his head grumpily.

The background information on Pernik that Coors had given me said that the old man was seventy-six and he looked it. He sat, leaning slightly forward in the chair, buttoned up to the neck with a gray woolen sweater, his long, bony legs encased in thick brown corduroy trousers.

He looked at each of us, taking his time, as if making individual assessments, and then raked us all with a glance that seemed to give him our collective worth. He grunted and looked up at his granddaughter. "Which is the leader, the handsome one over there?"

"That is Mr. Knight. Mr. St. Ives is at your right."

"Who is the woman?"

"She is Miss Tonzi of the American embassy."

"The other man?"

"A colleague of Mr. St. Ives. Mr. Wisdom."

"Hard names to remember," he said, turning his bald, pink head toward me. "I'm an old man," he rumbled in his harsh voice. "Why should anyone risk their lives for me? I didn't ask for it. They must be fools."

"I don't know," I said.

He pushed his metal-framed glasses up the wide bridge of his long, pink nose. "That ambassador of yours. He has a hard name too."

"Killingsworth," I said.

"Yes. Killingsworth. He came to see me many times. Brought things, books mostly. I was grateful. The man talked too much. Talked about himself. Now he has been—uh—stolen. No. It is another word. I can never remember it."

"Kidnapped," I said.

"Ah. Kid-napped. That is a good word. English, isn't it? I mean it's not American?"

"English first," I said.

"Well, how is he?"

"Killingsworth?"

"Yes. Is he safe? Have they killed him? I have heard that they do sometimes."

"I haven't heard from the kidnappers yet," I said.

"Damned fools, I say. I'm not sure I want to go to America. Sandburg's dead, isn't he?"

"Yes."

"I would have liked to have met him, talked to him. That old man Frost, he's dead, too, I hear."

"Yes, he's dead."

"I think I would have liked Sandburg better. He had more juice. How is my English?"

"It's fine."

"I knew it well once, perfectly some said. But we Slavs have an ear, you know," he said poking his right forefinger at his ear. "French, I know; German, too. I even learned Hungarian and only an idiot would attempt that if he's past twenty-five. I was. Impossible language. Impossible people." He seemed to drift off into some private memory for a moment. His granddaughter kept the conversation going.

"Are you acquainted with Mr. Killingsworth, Mr. St. Ives?" she said.

"Yes, I am."

"He was very kind to my grandfather. They had long talks."

"I suppose you got to know him well?" I said, deciding that that was as delicate a way to put it as any.

She smiled. "Not very. He was terribly polite, but I suppose most ambassadors are. He did give me a ride to market once in his little car. It was new then and he seemed very proud of it. I understand that it was the one he was driving when they kidnapped him near Sarajevo."

"You mean you don't know Mr. Killingsworth well?" I

said, proud of the way that I kept the astonishment out of my voice.

"My grandfather does, but I am sure Mr. Killingsworth thinks of me as a child."

"She is twenty-two," the old man said, rejoining us from wherever it was that he had been. He started to reminisce then about how it had been when he was twenty-two, but I didn't listen. I thought instead of Amfred Killingsworth, fifty, millionaire, publisher, and diplomat, who supposedly had turned his back on all of it for the love of a twenty-two-year-old girl who had once shared with him the deep intimacy of a ride to market in his little car which, if I knew Killingsworth, was an $8,000 Porsche.

Having met Gordana Panić, I could understand how any man, millionaire or not, might well toy with the idea of chucking it all, wife, kids, job, house and car, if she promised to join him on the next tramp leaving for Tahiti. Or a shyer man might simply worship her from afar, even if she were his secretary and worked in the next office. But Amfred Killingsworth was no shy dreamer. If he fell in love at fifty, he'd damn well make sure that the girl learned of it shortly after he'd told his lawyers to make all necessary legal arrangements.

So it seemed that either Killingsworth had lied to Coors, or Coors had lied to me, or Gordana Panić was the best liar of the lot.

"Have you seen Artur Bjelo lately?" I said to Gordana.

She shook her head slightly and smiled apologetically. "Is he from Belgrade?" she said. "The name is not at all familiar, but perhaps my grandfather knows him."

"Who? Who?" the old man rasped.

"Artur Bjelo," I said, raising my voice.

"No," he said, wagging his head. "How does he look?"

"He looks something like me," I said, "except younger. About ten years younger."

Pernik peered at me through his glasses and again shook his head slowly, so I gave up on that one and tried another. "Your fiancé must be concerned about your leaving for America," I said. "Does he plan to join you there?" I felt that no one would compliment me on my subtlety that afternoon.

Gordana Panić gave me another wondering smile and then blushed a little. She did it nicely. "I am not engaged, Mr. St. Ives, so there is no fiancé to worry about what I do."

"That's wonderful," Wisdom said.

The old man grinned at Wisdom. "You're not as handsome as that one," he said, nodding at Knight, "but at least you have a voice. That one has yet to utter a word. Can he not speak?"

"Yes, sir, I can," Knight said, turning on all of his considerable charm. "Words, in fact, are my trade, but I have none to describe your granddaughter's loveliness."

The old man chuckled again and looked at Gordana.

"She does have beauty, doesn't she? It's from her mother's family, not from mine. But if words are your trade, Mister—uh—"

"Knight."

"Yes, Knight. Then you must be a writer."

"An actor," Knight said.

"Oh," the old man said and turned back to Wisdom. "What might be your trade, sir?"

Wisdom smiled. "I'm a capitalist."

"Good," Pernik said as if he met one every day. "I'm a Royalist and I'm old enough not to care who knows it. But before I'm a Royalist, I'm a Croat, and before I'm a Croat,

I'm a Yugoslav. That's one thing about Tito. He's a Yugoslav first, even before he's a Croat. Or, I suspect, even a Bolshevik. But that's enough of that. Tell me what I can expect in America, young lady."

Arrie Tonzi grinned at him. "Too much of this and too little of that."

"That could be any country," he said, "which is reassuring. I don't wish to die in a country that is too different from my own."

"You are not to talk that way," Gordana said.

The old man shrugged. "Then if we cannot talk of death, and politics leads to argument, let's talk of what this young man wants us to do." He nodded at me.

"We haven't heard from the kidnappers yet," I said, "so I don't know when or where the exchange will take place. I suggest that you take with you only what you can carry. Perhaps the American embassy will see about forwarding your other possessions."

"Souvenirs mostly," Pernik said. "Not worth saving yet too precious to throw away. That's what souvenirs are."

"How much notice will we have, Mr. St. Ives?" Gordana asked.

"I don't know; possibly only a day or two, perhaps less, so I suggest that you have your bags packed. I already have the papers that will allow you to cross the border."

"Which border?" Pernik asked.

"Either into Italy or Austria. You will be accompanied by Mr. Knight and Mr. Wisdom."

He nodded and muttered good.

"They will not harm Mr. Killingsworth, will they?" Gordana asked.

"What bothers me," the old man interrupted, thumping

105

the arm of his chair, "is who these idiots could be. I can understand them asking for a million dollars. That's simple economics. You kidnap an ambassador and make sure that the ransom is in good hard currency. But who'd want an old, forgotten poet?" He brightened. "But perhaps it's not me. Perhaps it's Gordana whom they want." He turned toward his granddaughter and smiled. "If I did not know that you were already spoken for, Gordana, I might think you had a secret lover."

She blushed again and smiled, a little shyly.

"Spoken for?" I said.

"Since she was sixteen," the old man said, nodding happily.

"I thought she wasn't engaged."

"To the Church, Mr. St. Ives," he said proudly. "She's to be the bride of Him who is greater than us all."

"We were not to speak of it," Gordana said, even more shyly than before.

"She's just been waiting for me to die," he said, "before entering the sisterhood. Now she will do it in America."

"What a waste," Wisdom muttered.

Gordana said something to Pernik in Serbo-Croatian and the old man nodded vigorously. "My granddaughter reminds me that we have forgotten our hospitality. You will join us in a glass of brandy," he said. There was no question in his tone.

After the plum brandy was served, Gordana looked at me curiously and then once again spoke rapidly to her grandfather in Serbo-Croatian. The old man pulled his glasses down his nose and gazed at me over the rims. Then he pushed them back into place and gave me another hard stare.

"Forgive my rudeness, Mr. St. Ives, but Gordana just brought something to my attention." He took another sip of his brandy and stared at me some more, this time nodding his head affirmatively. "You remember asking if we knew a man called—uh—"

"Bjelo," his granddaughter said.

"Yes, if we knew a Bjelo who looked something like you. I know no one by that name but there was a young man who resembles you strongly whom we did once see quite often. Almost daily, in fact."

"The resemblance is really remarkable," Gordana said. "Except for the eyes. You have much kinder eyes."

"Who was he?" I said.

"His name was Stepinac. Arso Stepinac. He was about ten years younger than you, Mr. St. Ives. The fellow became quite boring with all of his questions."

"Questions?" I said.

"Yes," the old man said. "That was his job, to ask me questions."

"About what?"

Pernik made a broad gesture. "About life and love, of course, what else does one question a poet about, even a forgotten poet?"

"He asked my grandfather about politics and about his old friends," Gordana said. "The questioning went on almost daily for several weeks."

"When was this?" I said.

"A month or so ago," the old man said. "I haven't been questioned like that in years. And then one day, without any notice, Stepinac came no longer."

"Did you ever find out who he was or who he was with?" I said.

Pernik looked at me curiously. "Find out? There was nothing to find out. He told me. It was the first thing he told me.

I don't answer just anyone's questions, not day after day."

I sighed. "All right," I said. "Who was he?"

"Stepinac was younger than you, all right," the old man said, "but I don't know about the eyes. His seemed—well—steadier. Who was he? There's no secret. He was Arso Stepinac and he said he was an official or something with the UDBA, the State Security Police. I never did learn why he was questioning me."

CHAPTER **12**

They came for me at three o'clock in the morning. There was the knock at the door, loud enough for me to hear, but not so loud as to disturb the neighbors. Still, it disturbed Arrie Tonzi who rolled over in the bed and sleepily asked, "What time is it?"

"Three o'clock," I said, fumbling for my trousers. "Go back to sleep."

I still like to think that Arrie was in my bed at three o'clock that morning because my virtues were admirable, my personality engaging, and my charms irresistible. But it was probably because of the wine that we'd begun dinner with the night before. We had dined together alone in my room because I wanted to stay by the phone in case the kidnappers called and when I'd invited Arrie to join me, she accepted. Wisdom and Knight had gone off to explore Belgrade.

The wine had led to talk and the talk had led to shared intimacies which had led to that first, tentative embrace, the one where two lonely persons know they can stop if they want to, but neither of us had wanted to, so we had made love to each other pleasurably, fondly, tenderly, even humorously, and that had led to me groping for my trousers at three o'clock in the morning.

There were two of them at the door, but only one of them had a gun, an automatic whose make I didn't recognize. They were both young, in their mid-twenties, and the one with the automatic motioned me back into the room. I backed into it and they came in, closing the door behind them. The one without the gun said something in Serbo-Croatian and when it was apparent that I didn't understand him, he started making motions with his hands.

"He wants you to get dressed," Arrie said.

They turned towards the bed where she was sitting and the one with the gun grinned at her. She hadn't bothered to pull the sheet up any higher than her lap, but it seemed to concern the two young men more than it did her.

"I've figured out that he wants me to get dressed," I said. "Why don't you ask him what happens after I do?"

She said several sentences or a long paragraph in Serbo-Croatian to the pair and the one with the gun answered her briefly. "You're to go with them," she said. "They'll bring you back."

"Ask them why the gun," I said and before she could, I said, "Never mind, it's obvious. Ask when I'll be back."

I was putting on my shoes and socks when she said, "They say that you'll be back by four thirty."

"If I'm not," I said, "call the cops."

"You want me to call them anyway?"

"Tell those two that you will if I'm not back by four thirty."

She told them and I watched their reaction. The blond one

with the gun shrugged, but kept it pointed carelessly at me. The other one, who had brown hair, grinned at Arrie who drew the sheet up around her shoulders. Probably because she was cold.

"You don't seem very excited," she said to me in an accusing tone as I shrugged into my topcoat.

"Neither do you," I said.

"Maybe they're the kidnappers," she said.

"Ask them."

She asked them and they both looked puzzled and the one with the gun waved it at me. I nodded and smiled at him and said, "Excuse me." I crossed over to the bed and tilted Arrie's face up to mine and kissed her gently.

"I can call down to the desk and—" I interrupted her with another kiss.

"I think they speak English," I said, "and I don't think we're going near the desk."

"Why?"

"It snowed late last night, remember?"

"Yes."

I kissed her again and one of them grunted impatiently. I gave him a backhanded wave without turning. "Look at their boots," I said. "They're bone dry."

She peered around my shoulder. "By Jove, Holmes, you're right."

"As usual," I said and turned toward the door. The one without the gun opened it and all three of us went through it and turned left toward the stairs rather than right toward the elevator. We went up two flights of stairs, down the corridor, and stopped in front of a door. The man without the gun knocked twice and then pushed the door open. He gestured for me to go through and when I did, the first thing I saw was the man who couldn't make up his mind whether his name was Artur Bjelo or Arso Stepinac.

"I saw some old friends of yours yesterday," I said.

He remained seated in a chair by the writing desk and looked at me casually, as if I'd dropped by to borrow a cup of brown sugar. "Pernik," he said.

"And his granddaughter. I can see now why you wrote her all those letters. Congratulations. She's lovely."

He stood up and crossed to a window and looked out of it, his back to me. The two he had sent to fetch me were still in the room, the one with the gun by the door, the other one in a chair near the bath. The gun was no longer in sight.

"I am not engaged to Gordana Panić, Mr. St. Ives, and my name is not Artur Bjelo."

"Is it Arso Stepinac?"

He turned and nodded slightly. "When it suits me, it is."

"Why the brush at the Frankfurt airport?"

"Brush?"

"You know. The me no speaka the English routine."

"That should be obvious," he said. "I wanted to avoid being seen with you."

"By whom?"

"I don't think that matters. Not to you."

"All right," I said. "I'll try another one. Who attempted to run you down in New York?"

He smiled and it was the familiar boyish grin, but I was sure he would smile just that same way when he was sixty, if he lived that long, but it wouldn't mean anything then either. "I've wondered about that," he said. "It may have been that someone mistook me for you, Mr. St. Ives. You've probably remarked our resemblance. Curious, isn't it?"

It was also curious that his English was better than it had been when I first met him.

"And you think that someone was after me?"

He shrugged. "It must be."

I decided to try a pre-prebreakfast cigarette and fumbled in my pockets for it without success. "You have a cigarette?" I said to Stepinac, but before he had a chance to say no the man with the gun was at my elbow offering me one of his, along with a light.

I looked at him. "You speak English after all," I said.

He smiled slightly. "A little. Your friend is very nice, yes?"

"Yes," I said.

"Do you know Miss Tonzi well?" Stepinac asked.

"Is that supposed to be a remark or a question?"

"Yes," he said and nodded apologetically. "I did not put it too well considering the circumstances. What I meant to ask is, did your Mr. Coors brief you on Miss Tonzi? Your instructions did come from Coors, we know that."

"Who's we?"

"Really, Mr. St. Ives, we seem to do nothing other than supply questions as answers to each other's questions."

"I'm sorry as hell," I said, "but that's how I answer questions at three o'clock in the morning after I'm rousted out of bed at the point of a gun by somebody I know nothing about except that he tells an awful lot of lies. But I'll answer one of your questions, the one about Arrie Tonzi. The answer's no, no one briefed me about her, no one called Coors or anything else, and if you think you're going to add to my day by telling me that she's a top U.S. agent, what the hell else do you think I expected to be saddled with on a deal like this? If she is an agent, I don't care which outfit she's with—State, CIA or what have you. I don't even know if she's tops; she may be just mediocre, but you'd know more about that than I do and you'd certainly care a hell of a lot more."

After I'd finished, Stepanic looked a bit discomfited, but he overcame it with his ever ready smile, remarking, "She's CIA, but very junior."

"What kind of a cop are you?" I said.

"You're certain that I am one?"

"We're back to questions to questions," I said. "Of course, I'm sure. Nobody but a cop would try that jilted lover routine that you tried on me in New York. I'll admit that your poet act's not bad."

"Well, we can only try, can't we, Mr. St. Ives? That's why we're seeing each other this morning. Again I'm going to try to convince you to delay the exchange of Anton Pernik and his granddaughter for your ambassador."

"For how long?" I said.

"Five days. No more."

"What happens then?"

"That is not your concern."

"It's out of my hands."

"I don't understand."

"Sure you do. I'm in sellers' market and when the kidnappers offer I have to buy or it may not be offered again. If I stall, they may grow suspicious, and if they grow suspicious, Ambassador Killingsworth might never be heard from again. And if that happened, I'd have nobody to blame but you, but you'd have what you wanted because the exchange of Pernik and his granddaughter would be delayed not for five days, but forever."

"You have a very suspicious mind."

I nodded. "That's right, I do, and that's because most of my business associates are either policemen or thieves. It

114

would make anyone suspicious, just like you make me suspicious. Guess what I did when you left my hotel in New York?"

"You called the delegation at the United Nations to see if an Artur Bjelo was employed there. They said no, of course."

"Anton Pernik says that you're a cop and that you're with the UDBA. What if I called them and asked if they happen to have an Arso Stepinac on the payroll?"

Stepinac smiled at the suggestion. "I would strongly advise you not to do that, Mr. St. Ives."

"All right," I said. "I won't. What's next, the threat?"

"I'm sorry."

"It seems logical enough. Since I've refused to stall the kidnapping exchange, you make a threat, preferably a dire one."

Stepinac turned and walked over to the window again and looked out at the weather. "I think you're forgetting something," he said.

"What?"

"Money."

"You're right," I said, "I did forget that. It's not like me."

"Are you very expensive, Mr. St. Ives?"

"I don't think you can afford me."

"I could offer you ten thousand pounds."

"Don't."

"It would not interest you?"

"Ten thousand pounds always interests me," I said. "But what I have to do to earn it doesn't."

"You really have to do nothing."

That's what a broker in Cleveland had said to me once. I'd been called in to buy back a half million dollars' worth of stolen negotiable securities for the bargain basement price of $100,000. It had gone smoothly and as the broker was counting out the securities on his desk, he'd said, "Insurance is a wonderful thing, isn't it?" Before I could agree with him he'd gone on to say, "If something had gone wrong and the thieves hadn't shown up, I would have been fully covered." He'd counted out $50,000 worth of securities and pushed them toward me. Then he'd looked at me, much as Stepinac was looking at me now, trying to gauge whether he'd placed too low a price on whatever it was he was trying to buy, my integrity, I suppose, perhaps my conscience, or maybe just my silent acquiescence, which, in the broker's opinion, wasn't worth more than $50,000 because, after all, as he'd said, "You don't really have to do anything."

He had been right, of course, and so was Stepinac. I didn't have to kill anyone or steal anything. All I had to do was lie a little, and that was painless, especially for me, and after I was through lying I would be richer by $50,000 or £10,000 or whatever my going rate was and none would be the wiser.

"You hesitate, Mr. St. Ives," Stepinac said. "Is my offer too low?"

I sighed and looked around for an ashtray. "No," I said, "it's just that my price is too high."

Stepinac nodded and said, "Your answer has some interesting overtones and it's too bad that we don't have more time to explore them. We Serbs are partial to such discussions. In fact, you may have noticed, even in your short time here, that we enjoy any kind of a discussion, regardless of topic."

"I've noticed," I said.

Stepinac walked over to the writing desk, picked up a sheet of paper, looked at it, put it down, and then tapped his lower lip thoughtfully. The man with the gun yawned and looked at his watch. The man in the chair by the bath caught the yawn and repeated it. Stepinac turned back toward me and I could see that he had another question.

"Do you take pride in this profession of yours, Mr. St. Ives?"

"Pride?"

"Yes, pride. Do you ever sense a feeling of accomplishment after one of your successful negotiations, a feeling of craftsmanship perhaps?"

"Pride's too weighty a word," I said. "Satisfaction's better, I suppose, but there's no feeling of creative accomplishment, if that's what you mean."

"Nothing like that felt by the artisan, or the lawyer, or the artist, or the doctor?"

"Or the cop?"

"Yes," he said, not smiling, "even the cop."

"I perform what should be an unneeded service," I said. "That rules out pride, right there."

"An unneeded service," Stepinac said thoughtfully, and then, catching the scent of a discussion, added, "If you wish to carry that to a philosophical extreme, a doctor, a lawyer, even a policeman performs the same thing."

"No," I said. "Doctors and lawyers and policemen would be unnecessary only if we lived in a moral and physical Utopia. That's still a few years off. A go-between is called in when the victim and the representatives of the system, usually the police, agree that the system's broken down and that they must operate outside of its framework for a while. So a go-between is hired and the rules are suspended while he does his job. Afterwards, the rules are reinstated and the system again tries to catch and punish whoever violated its rules. So I work only outside the system and only when its

117

rules have been suspended. You don't find much recognition in that territory, and pride or sense of accomplishment is usually dependent upon recognition of some sort."

Stepinac tapped his lower lip again. "Then why do you do it if it offers none of the usual rewards? Not for financial gain, surely. You can make as much at some less bizarre occupation."

"Money's only part of it," I said. "I'm lazy and this way I don't have to work too hard or too often. I can usually choose or reject my employer, depending upon whether his problem interests me. There's no competition and that's good for a man who has no ambition. And then it might be that I like other persons' troubles better than my own."

"Interesting," Stepinac said, picked up the sheet of paper from the writing table again, glanced at it, and put it down. "I was hoping that I might bribe you, Mr. St. Ives," he said. "I seem to have failed."

"It could be that you didn't try hard enough."

He smiled boyishly. "Somehow I don't think so, which is to your credit, of course. Now I must employ another method to delay the exchange."

"What?"

"I can't tell you. However, what I'm about to say is not a threat, dire or otherwise."

"All right."

"And I'll apologize in advance for its melodramatic note."

"Fine."

"It's only this, Mr. St. Ives. Before the week is over you will wish you had taken the bribe. Good night."

Arrie was up and pacing the floor when I got back to my room.

"Who was it?" she said.

"Nobody you know."

"What did they want?"

"They want me to delay the exchange."

"Why?"

"They didn't say."

"Jesus, what *did* they say?"

"That you work for the CIA."

"Oh."

"Let's go back to bed," I said.

"They know," she said. "Huh."

I unbuttoned my shirt. "Didn't you expect them to?"

"Oh, I don't know," she said. "What did you say?"

"When they told me?"

"Yes."

"I told them I didn't mind—that you probably needed the job."

CHAPTER 13

The call from the kidnappers came through at 11:05 that morning and the one who did the talking sounded Italian and spoke English with an American accent, but since World War II most of them speak it that way.

"We can't talk over this phone," he said.

"I agree."

"At eleven thirty a note's gonna be delivered to you at the hotel. Be at the hotel desk to get it in person. It'll tell you what to do. Okay?"

"Okay," I said.

"Okay," he said and hung up.

At eleven thirty I was strolling up and down before the hotel desk trying to pick out the plainclothesmen in the Metropol lobby. There were two possibles and three probables. A taxi driver came in and handed an envelope over to the desk clerk who glanced at it, nodded at me, and smiled when

I thanked him for it. The taxi driver looked surprised when he was led off by two men, one of whom I'd scored as a possible, the other as a probable.

I went back up to my room to read the note. It was hand lettered—printed would be better—with a ballpoint pen and it said: "Be at public phone at NE corner Strosmajerova and Risanska near central train station at one sharp! Don't be followed!! Burn this!!!"

All right!!! I thought and spent a few moments trying to memorize the street names before I gave up, located them on a city map, and marked the location with a big, black X. I used the toilet to dispose of the note.

I called Henry Knight and he sounded sleepy when he answered the phone. "How was your night on the town?" I said.

"Wicked," he said. "Wisdom is a bottomless pit and this morning I'm dying and nobody cares."

"Have some breakfast. They called."

"When?"

"A few minutes ago. I have to go out."

"You want some company?"

"Not yet. Maybe later this afternoon."

"I'll have recovered."

"Tell Wisdom to stick around, too."

"Anything else?"

"No," I said and hung up.

When I'd come out of the shower that morning Arrie was dressed and drinking a cup of coffee. "I think you should know," she said, "that I don't consider last night to be just part of my job."

121

"I don't care about your job," I said, kissed her, and poured a cup of coffee. "I really don't. I told you that."

"I've started to like you, Phil," she said. "I mean honestly."

"If we like each other, we're off to a head start."

"You're not pissed off?" Her swearing had become an unconscious habit and the words that she once may have used for shock value were now just part of her vocabulary. I didn't mind; the language is going to hell anyway.

"Not in the least," I said and rumpled her hair which looked much the same when I was done. She gave it a couple of quick strokes with a comb, but it was like combing a blond mop.

"Well," she said, "they must not think you're too terribly important. Or something."

"Why?"

"Not if they put me on to you."

"What is it that you're really supposed to do, take notes or arrive in the nick of time?"

She shrugged. "I just give them a daily report on whom you see and what you say. That's all." She lifted her face to be kissed again and what started as a breakfast peck turned into something more interesting. "You're sexy in the morning," she said. "I like that."

"Which still leaves the afternoon to be explored."

"I have to go," she said, slipping into her long suede coat.

"Who's your relief?" I said, grinning at her. "Something tall and brunette with a throaty voice and wicked eyes?"

She made a face at me. "If there is one, they haven't told me. But that wouldn't be unusual. I'm sort of junior junior."

"You're still the only one."

"Only what?"

I grinned at her once more. "The only CIA agent I ever made love to."

The weather had cleared, the temperature had climbed up to the low thirties, and I decided to walk to the corner of Strosmajerova and Risanska because it didn't seem to be a mile, if that, and I needed the time to think and also to make sure that I wasn't followed!

I started out briskly enough, with a healthy 120 paces a minute, and by the time I'd gone a block I'd spotted both of them. One was a pale blond man in a dark overcoat and a fur hat who preferred the opposite side of the street. The other was shorter, a little stout, and looked as if he might be puffing a bit to keep up the pace. Neither of them were experts, not according to the surveillance standards of a retired New York private detective who'd written a book on the subject that no one would publish. He had once spent a patient week teaching me how to spot and lose a tail in exchange for my editorial advice, which had been to send him to an agent who'd sold excerpts from the book to various law and order magazines.

One of these fine days, I promised myself as I crossed Marsala Tita near the Drama Theater, I would take up a trade that could be conducted entirely by mail. I might become a stamp dealer. If I had to deal with liars, their lies (as well as my own) would have to be written down and there's something forbidding about committing a lie to paper, although it probably wouldn't bother Hamilton Coors too much.

I headed diagonally across a large park toward Nemanjina Street. The park was crisscrossed with walks from which the snow had been carefully removed for those who liked to stroll through it in mid-February. Other than myself and my two shadowers there were only three other strollers and they all looked as if they were using the park as a shortcut.

After trying to guess how many lies Coors had told me, I started to wonder again whether Amfred Killingsworth was really smitten by the twenty-two-year-old beauty whose grandfather-poet wasn't at all sure that he wanted to go to America, now that Sandburg was dead. Although the U.S. Department of State seemed to know all about its ambassador's passionate love for Gordana Panić, a love that had caused him to balk at his recall, Killingsworth apparently had forgotten to tell the girl about it, unless she and her grandfather were both lying about her plans to become a Catholic nun.

And then there was my look-alike, Arso Stepinac, who wanted me to delay the kidnap exchange for five days so that he could do something or other that he thought needed to be done. All that Jovan Tavro, with his sad carp face and his roses and his bitterness, wanted to do during those same five days was to stay alive until I could whisk him out of the country, probably under the noses of Stepinac and Slobodan Bartak, the ambitious, pint-size official in the Ministry of Interior who thought it would have been nice of me to double-cross the kidnappers. I speculated about whether Stepinac and Bartak knew each other and, if they did, whether they were working together or at cross purposes. The more I thought about it the more it didn't really seem to matter.

By the time I came into view of the Hotel Astoria I was wondering about whether the CIA had taught Arrie Tonzi how to cook and by then it was time to get rid of my two tails.

"All hotels have basements," the retired private detective

had told me. "All basements have rear exits. So you go up, then down, then out."

I went into the lobby of the Hotel Astoria, bought a package of Morava cigarettes for three dinars, lit one, and watched my two tails try to look unobtrusive as they entered and headed for opposite ends of the lobby. I went over to the room clerk, asked him what time it was, and then headed for the elevator. When it came, I saw my two escorts moving toward the room clerk.

I took the elevator up to the third floor, got out and walked down the service stairs to the basement which also contained the kitchen. That was even better. I nodded to the chef and his assistants as I went through the kitchen to the door that inevitably had to lead up to the alley and the trash cans. I took the alley until it ended on Gavrila Principa and turned right. Another block of quick walking and I was at the phone booth at Sarajevska and Nemanjina.

It was still cold and I had to stand around stamping my feet until it rang at exactly one o'clock. I picked it up and said hello and the Italian-American voice said, "You sure you weren't followed?"

"I made sure," I said. "When can I talk to Killingsworth?"

"Whaddya wanta talk to him for?"

"Did you take a look at this morning's papers?"

"No, I didn't take a look at this morning's papers."

"My picture's in them. Also my name. It's all about how I'm going to hand over a million dollars for Killingsworth. So how do I know you didn't pick my name out of the paper and decide to make yourself a quick million?"

"Ah, hell," he said, "there ain't no million dollars."

"That's all I wanted to hear you say," I said. "Now where's Killingsworth?"

"We got him in a castle."

"A castle?"

"Well, it used to be a castle, but now it's more like a hunting lodge."

"Who owns it?"

"Well, that depends. It used to belong to some Hungarian count before the war and after that he claimed to have sold it to a Greek businessman, but the government moved in and used it as a school for a while, so the Greek's relatives are suing the government, but they're not getting anywhere, so now nobody's using it, especially in winter, because the only way you can get to it is by horseback."

"Where is it?"

"About thirty-five kilometers southeast of Sarajevo."

"How do I get there?"

"I'll have to meet you in Sarajevo."

"When?"

"The sooner the better. The ambassador's getting tired of it."

"Tired of what?"

"Chopping wood. We need a lot of wood to keep warm and it keeps him quiet."

"All right. Name where and when."

"Saturday. You know Sarajevo?"

I sighed. "No, I don't know Sarajevo."

"Well, there's a gypsy quarter there called Dajanil Osmanbeg. It's in a suburb called Bistrik. I'll meet you there at nine Saturday night in the old railway station."

"How'll you recognize me?"

"I'll buy a copy of today's paper."

"There'll be five of us," I said. "Four men and a woman."

He muttered a curse in Serbo-Croatian or, for all I knew, in Macedonian. "That means six horses," he said.

"From Sarajevo?"

"No, we'll take a car out of there. But there's still five kilometers that you can only make with a horse unless you want to walk and I understand Pernik's pretty old."

"Try for the horses," I said.

"Can you ride?"

"No, but I can hang on."

"They'll be wooden saddles."

"I prefer western," I said.

"What?"

"Never mind."

"Okay," he said. "Nine o'clock at the railway station. You got where it is?"

"Near the gypsy quarter, Dajanil Osmanbeg," I said. "In Bistrik, a suburb of Sarajevo."

"That's pretty good. It's not quite the right accent, but it's pretty good."

"I studied at Linguaphone," I said.

"What?"

"It must be the connection."

"One more thing," he said.

"What?"

"Don't be followed!"

"I won't!" I said and hung up.

I crossed the street and headed up Gavrila Principa again, turned left into the alley, made my way around the trash cans, went down the flight of steps that led to the entrance of the kitchen, nodded at the chef who nodded back this time, walked up the stairs to the third floor, caught the elevator down to the lobby, and went over to the desk clerk and said, "I'm expecting to meet some friends here. Has anybody been asking for Mr. St. Ives?"

He swallowed a couple of times and then nervously pointed to the two who'd followed me from the Metropol hotel and who now looked as if they were trying to blend with the wallpaper.

"Would these be the gentlemen?" he said.

I looked at the blond one, who looked away, and then at the short, stocky one who suddenly busied himself with a hangnail. "No," I said, loudly enough for them both to hear, "I'm afraid I don't know these gentlemen."

CHAPTER **14**

I had been talking for almost half an hour. My throat was dry and scratchy so I decided to try some of the plum brandy that I had bought on my way back from the Hotel Astoria. Park Wisdom shuddered as I drank it. We were in my room and he was slumped in a chair by the window, a trifle pale, more than a little wan. Henry Knight was stretched out on the bed, staring at the ceiling. He looked better than Wisdom, but almost anyone could have.

"Where does it hurt?" I said to Wisdom who smiled feebly.

"Do you remember your *pas de deux* with the belly dancer?" Knight said to the ceiling.

"I thought your one-man revival of *The Glass Menagerie* was more interesting," Wisdom said to the window.

"We made a lot of friends during the evening," Knight said.

"Fostered understanding," Wisdom said. "Gained valuable insight, too."

"Oh, Christ, I'm dying," Knight said.

"It's my turn on the bed," Wisdom said. "Die in a chair."

"Sure you wouldn't care for a drop?" I said, offering the bottle around.

Knight groaned, swung his feet to the floor and pushed himself up. Wisdom rose gingerly and walked slowly to the bed. Knight eased himself into the chair by the window and Wisdom carefully lowered himself onto the bed. "When do you want me to rent the car?" he said.

"Now," I said. "This afternoon. Go for a drive, the fresh air will give you a reason for living."

"And you think we might be followed?" Knight said.

"Don't worry about it."

"I can't," he said. "I can only suffer."

"You're seeing who this afternoon?" Wisdom said.

"Bill Jones."

"Bill Jones," he said. "What a nice, simple name. He's probably looking forward to a quiet evening at hearthside surrounded by his family. He feels no pain. He suffers no remorse. I wish my name were Bill Jones."

"Who do you think might follow us?" Knight said. "Friends of that guy who looks like you or friends of the other one from the Ministry of Interior, what's his name—"

"Slobodan Bartak," Wisdom said. "He doesn't have a nice, simple name."

"Either or both," I said. "But it doesn't matter. Just give them a nice, long ride."

"There'll be trouble in the Balkans come spring, gentlemen," Wisdom said to the ceiling. "Mark my word."

"Do you mean war, Sir Malcolm?" Knight said.

"Only needs a spark, Worlington-Hoopes."

"To ignite the tinderbox of Europe," Knight said.

"Damned fine phrase, Worlington-Hoopes. Yours?"

"Go rent the car," I said.

At the door, Wisdom turned and said, "What time are you seeing Grandpa Pernik?"

"Arrie set the appointment up for five."

"When you see Gordana," he said, "tell her, well, you know, tell her that I love her."

"You've recovered," I said.

I used the garage exit of the Metropol to avoid being followed, caught a rare, government-owned taxi at the main post office, and handed the driver the address that Tavro had written down. It was another trip through blocks of buildings and apartments that seemed to fall into three distinct styles: early Hapsburg, with all of Vienna's turgid froth, but none of its charm; late Stalinoid, grim and stark enough to create galloping paranoia; and what I suppose could be called Enlightened Revisionism which had a lot of glass and aluminum and colored panels and whose twin could be found near any good-sized shopping center on the outskirts of Kansas City.

The driver stopped before a small old house on a block that the Nazi bombers seemed to have missed which was about three miles from the center of Belgrade. It was a short narrow street and the houses that nestled along the edge of the sidewalk had a turn of the century air about them. They were built of dark brown brick and varied in height from two to four stories. The house that the driver kept pointing at was a three-story building with two dormer windows and a tiled, dark red roof. I could see no house number, but I paid the driver what was on the meter and his socialist conscience didn't object to the tip.

The sun was out although it was still cold. Three cats, one tortoiseshell and two tabbies, sat on the third riser of the

131

stone steps that led to the door and washed themselves and blinked at the sun and yawned at each other. They looked well fed.

I knocked on the door and when no one answered, I knocked again. The door opened about six inches and a woman's face looked out at me. She had gray hair. "Mr. Jones," I said. She nodded and then closed the door. I waited. The door opened wide this time and a man dressed in blue Levis and a gray work shirt looked at me with calm, dark brown eyes. He was taller than I, more than six feet, and he had broad heavy shoulders and a bull chest and almost no hips that I could see. His dark hair was sparse on top and he wore it full at the sides where its gray ends lapped and curled over the tops of his long ears.

"I'm looking for Bill Jones," I said.

"I'm Jones," he said in a deep grating voice whose harsh vibrato threatened to rattle the windows. "You're the American."

"St. Ives," I said. "Philip St. Ives."

He nodded and then, almost as an afterthought, held out his right hand. It was a big, hard hand, but he didn't use it to show how tough he was. He wouldn't need to. When I was inside he kept the door ajar and said something in soft Serbo-Croatian. The three cats scampered in and trotted down a hall toward the rear of the house.

"Belong to the kids," Jones said gruffly. We went into a sitting room and he waved me to an overstuffed chair that was covered with a worn plum-colored fabric. It matched the sofa that Jones lowered himself into. There were some crude oils on the walls of mountain scenes, along with the stuffed heads of a large buck and a wild-eyed wolf. There was also a framed photograph of some smiling men in various uniforms

132

in what looked to be a forest setting who toasted the camera with their canteen cups. They had rifles and submachine guns slung over their shoulders. A white tile stove gave off heat in one corner. The floor was covered with dark Oriental rugs.

Jones sat on the couch, leaning forward, his forearms resting on his knees. He had a careful, watchful face, heavy-chinned and full-lipped, with a blunt, strong nose and a deep, frowning V between his thick eyebrows. Harsh lines, almost furrows, formed trenches around his mouth. I judged him to be somewhere between fifty and fifty-five.

"You want to get in touch with Tavro," he said, making it a statement. "When?"

"Tonight."

He nodded. "Okay. I'll get word to him. You want to meet at that same place?"

"The Impossible?"

He nodded.

"That's fine," I said.

"What time?"

"Late. Around ten."

He nodded again as the gray-haired woman came in carrying a beaten brass tray with three cups and three glasses on it. The tortoiseshell cat followed her into the room and jumped up on Jones's lap. He stroked its head with one large hand and it turned on its purring machine. "This is the wife," Jones said as the woman offered me the coffee and slivovica. "She doesn't speak much English." He said something in Serbo-Croatian and the woman smiled at me. Despite the gray hair and drab dress, she was glowingly attractive and it was obvious that she once had been pretty, perhaps even beautiful. I said thank you and she smiled again and then served Jones.

"You've been here a long time, I understand," I said.

"Since forty-eight," he said. "It was as soon as I could get back in. We got married then."

"Have you been back to the States since?"

"No, but I got a kid over there now, my oldest boy. He's going to Brown on a scholarship." He paused to drain his slivovica in a quick gulp. "Tavro told you about me being with the Partisans, didn't he?"

"He mentioned it."

"They parachuted me in. September of forty-four."

"OSS?"

His eyes narrowed slightly, some, but not much. "Yeah, OSS. I was a radio man, but the radio got busted in the drop so they handed me a machine gun instead. That's what I did until it was over. I met Roza here Christmas Day, 1944." His wife brightened and smiled at the sound of her name. She sat in a straight-backed chair, her feet barely touching the floor, and sipped her coffee and plum brandy, politely following the conversation with her eyes, if not with her ears.

"Where'd you know Tavro?" I said.

"*U šume*—in the woods," Jones said. "He was Rankovic's dog robber. We got to know each other pretty well and we've kept in touch over the years. We've gone hunting some together. He was with me when I got that wolf up there."

"He told you I'm getting him out," I said.

Jones gave me a long, level stare before he replied. "He told me that you were going to try."

"He says he's afraid of being killed."

Once again Jones was silent before he made his comment, as if he had only so many phrases to spend and he didn't want

134

to part with any of them carelessly. "He's a Serb," he said finally.

"What's that mean?"

Jones turned his heavy head toward his wife and spoke to her in Serbo-Croatian. She smiled, nodded, gathered up our glasses and cups on the tray, and headed toward the rear of the house. The cat jumped off Jones's lap and followed her, its tail a moving exclamation mark. "She's a Serb, too," Jones said. "If I asked her how were things in town today, she might say fine, and let it go at that, or she might take the rest of the afternoon to tell me, part of the time laughing about what happened and part of the time crying, even if she did no more than buy some thread. But if she's in the mood, she can make buying a spool of thread a hell of an adventure that's full of all sorts of meaning. If she's in the mood and most of the time, being a Serb, she is. Tavro's like that."

"You mean he's not in any danger?"

"I mean he's a Serb and if he thinks he's in danger of being killed, he likes to talk about it. But that doesn't mean he isn't. I think he is, but then I'm just a construction worker."

"Why?"

"You mean why do I think he's in danger?"

"That's right."

"You follow the politics here closely?"

"Some."

"You remember in sixty-six when they were talking about a public trial for Rankovic?"

"Yes."

"But nothing came of it?"

"Yes."

"You know why?"

"Not really."

135

"Well, one, it would be like putting the American Secretary of State on trial. What's his name—uh—"

"Rogers."

"Rogers, yeah. I keep thinking Rusk, but it's Rogers now. But it would be like putting Rusk or Rogers on trial for treason. That's one. Now suppose Rusk or Rogers was not only Secretary of State, but also head of the FBI and the CIA combined. What if he was that?"

"I thought Rankovic was vice-president."

"He was, but what the hell does an American vice-president do?"

"You're right."

"So what if it was like I said."

"It would scare Congress silly," I said.

"Especially if it was brought out that the Secretary of State had bugged not only the White House, but also the offices and homes of the entire cabinet and had it fixed up so that he could listen in on all their phone calls from his own bedroom."

"Is that what the setup was?"

"The big shots live out in a fancy Belgrade suburb called Dedinje. Rankovic lived at twenty-five Uzicka Street. The telephone system was rigged so that he was tapped into any house that had a lower number than his. Tito's address is fifteen Uzicka. Hell, there was even a tap on the phone in Tito's bedroom. It was all in the papers. So they kicked Rankovic out of the party, fired him as vice-president and head of the UDBA, but refused to give him a public trial. Guess why?"

"He might embarrass somebody."

"Enough to fill a graveyard. Everything they accused Rankovic of doing, they'd done, too, and that means kickbacks, importing cars tax free and then selling them, letting the government pay for their fancy villas, operating private gambling joints, even using convict labor. You name it. Rankovic had the goods on them and when he wasn't monitoring those phones, guess who was?"

"Tavro," I said.

"That's right."

"And he knows all the dirt."

"Most of it anyway."

"So somebody's scared that he'll talk."

"They should be."

"But it all happened in 1966," I said.

Jones took his time to remove a cigarette from a leather case. He looked at it, rolled it in his fingers, and then lit it with a match. "Tito was born in 1892," he said. "How much longer you give him?"

"I see what you mean."

"It's a nice job," Jones said, "and a lot of people want it. Now if you thought you might be in line for it, and there was somebody around who might know something that would embarrass you, you might just make a wish that this person would disappear."

And if a certain government had this information, I thought, and used it discreetly and wisely, it could help determine who would, or would not, head the pecking order in Yugoslavia once its uncontested leader was no longer Josip Broz Tito. Of course, things would fall apart if this same information were to be prematurely spread across the front page of a large American newspaper that just happened to be owned by the U.S. Ambassador to Yugoslavia. If that danger threatened, you just might do something to prevent it. You might even kidnap your own ambassador.

137

I suddenly realized that Jones was looking at me expectantly. "I said do you want another drink?" he said.

"No thanks."

"I'll get word to Tavro."

I rose. "Any idea of where I can get a cab?"

He shook his head. "Not much chance around here and I haven't got a phone. I'll walk you to the bus."

I smiled and said good-bye to Mrs. Jones as her husband slipped into a heavy gray overcoat. He said something to her in Serbo-Croatian and she nodded and smiled at me and said, "Good-bye." It may have been the only English she knew.

"You ever think of going back to the States?" I said as we walked down the narrow street.

"Not much," Jones said. "She has her family here and I don't have anyone but a brother, so it doesn't make much sense. But it was rough at first."

"How do you mean?"

"They didn't know what to make of me. They must have had me followed for two years. There was a hell of a mess about work permits and so on. I'm just lucky that I own half a farm in Nebraska or we might have starved. My brother sent me my share. Finally, Tavro got Rankovic to put a stop to it. They just think I'm the nutty American now."

"You like it here, huh?"

He smiled at me. It was a curious smile, tinged with a kind of sad pride. "I like my wife and you can't beat the fishing," he said. "But it wasn't all my idea."

We crossed the street and turned left. "Whose was it?"

"You can catch the bus here," he said. "It'll take you to the Trg Republike and you can catch a cab or walk from there."

"Whose idea was it?" I said again.

He looked at me and then cleared his throat magnificently in true Yugoslav fashion and spat in the gutter. "Washington's," he said. "I'm supposed to be a sleeper. You know what a sleeper is?"

I told him that I did and he nodded. "Yeah, I thought that you might. Well, that was twenty-three years ago and I was young then. But I'm older now and since I haven't heard a word in all that time you might just tell them something for me if you ever get the chance when you're back in Washington."

"What?"

"Tell them not to wake me up." He nodded brusquely, turned, and walked off down the street.

CHAPTER 15

At five o'clock that afternoon I was knocking on the door of Anton Pernik's apartment under the expectant gaze of one of the plainclothes guards who was far more interested in getting a look at Gordana Panić than he was in me.

He gave her his best smile when she opened the door, but she didn't smile back. She looked at me for a long moment and said, "Come in, Mr. St. Ives. You're just in time."

I followed her into the sitting room. She turned to survey it and then pointed at the large chair where her grandfather had held forth when I'd been there the first time.

"Sit there," she said, "it's comfortable. I'll get us some brandy."

She disappeared through a door and I looked around the room and it seemed much the same. The pictures of the men with their high collars and their slicked-back hair were still on the walls. The books were still behind the glass doors of their cases.

If anything had changed, it was Gordana. She had on a different dress, a dark red one that was shorter than the one she'd worn previously; but anyone can wear a new dress. Not everyone can wear a new mood that is so pronounced that it manifests a noticeably different personality.

When she came back with the brandy I said, "How is your grandfather?"

She didn't answer until she served the drinks and was sitting in a straight-backed chair next to mine, the same one she had sat in during my other visit. I had to turn slightly to see her. She looked at me over the rim of her glass. "He's been detained," she said.

"Will he be back soon?" I said.

"No," she said, "not soon."

"I've heard from the kidnappers," I said.

"Yes," she said and drained her brandy. Her answer wasn't quite what I expected.

"They want to exchange Killingsworth tomorrow night. In a place near Sarajevo."

"I think I would like another brandy," she said. "Would you care for one?"

"Why not?" I said and watched her move across the room. There seemed to be a difference in the way she walked, but it could have been the shorter dress. Maybe it was the brandy. I looked around the room again and I knew how it had changed. Nothing had been added, but something had been taken away. All the religious artifacts—the crosses, the paintings of Jesus and Mary, a carved ivory representation of the crucifixion, agonizing in its detail, and a number of other religious oils were gone, leaving pale outlines of where they had hung against the darker wallpaper.

When Gordana came back with the brandy, I said, "I see

you've moved some things around. Are you thinking of taking them with you?"

She looked around the room, sipped her brandy, and nodded vaguely. "I moved them," she said, adding, "to a more appropriate room." Once more she looked at me over the rim of her glass. "Are you a religious person, Mr. St. Ives?"

"Not terribly," I said. "Hardly at all, in fact."

"Are you an atheist like Tito?"

"I don't know," I said.

"But you are not a Catholic?"

"No."

"If someone asked what your nationality was, what would you say?"'

I looked at her. She had finished her second glass of brandy and she was smiling at me. It was a mischievous smile, but the look in her eyes was more than that. It was wicked.

"I'd say American, I guess. Or United States citizen."

"But you have fifty states. Would you not say New Yorker or California-uh-an? Is that right?"

"That's right, but I wouldn't say that. I wouldn't even say Ohioan, although that's where I was born."

"If you asked anyone in this country what they were, they would say Serb or Croat or Slovene or Montenegran. I think Gospodin Tito is our only true Yugoslav, but then he's only half Croat. His mother was a Slovene."

"What would you call yourself?" I said.

"I would call myself Gospodin Gordana," she said, rising. She twirled and her red skirt twirled with her, giving me a fine full view of what I was sure were the world's most beautiful legs. "Citizen Gordana," she said, holding her glass aloft, "citizen of the world."

142

"Nice," I said, referring to her legs, but indicating the plum brandy.

"Would you like some more?"

"What are we celebrating?" I said.

She put her glass down and grasped the two arms of my chair and leaned forward until her face was close to mine. Very close. A quick glance down assured me that she, too, had joined the no-bra league. I had a hard time deciding where to rest my eyes, but finally decided on her face which was lovely and interesting and, after all, very close to mine. It would have been impolite not to.

"We are celebrating, Gospodin St. Ives, *me!*"

Well, there wasn't anything else to do so I did it. I kissed her. She knew how to do it. Her tongue darted into my mouth, seeking, caressing, a warm, wet determined explorer. I soon found that she wore nothing under her dress and that her skin was as smooth and delightful to touch as it was to look at. Her hands got busy too and then we were naked on the floor and all over each other, feverishly probing, tasting, and demanding from each other. Nobody gave very much; it was all take, and at that particular time and place it was the way we both wanted it and so that's what we did. And then she gave a half scream, cutting it off by sinking her teeth into my shoulder as her hips arched high and hard into mine and her nails raked my back. She shuddered violently, once, twice, and then she was pounding her body against mine again and gasping, shuddering once again, but less violently, and then subsiding slowly, quietly.

We lay there on the Oriental rugs, thinking our own thoughts. I memorized a pattern in one of the rugs. She ran her fingers down the side of my neck. I propped myself up on my elbows and studied her. There was a warm, sexual glow about Gordana that made her indescribably beautiful, but that's all. Earlier that day, I had looked at another girl who had that same glow, but who was not nearly so beautiful, not half, who had hair that flopped around over a pert, saucy face and I had felt something, tenderness, affection, care. Something. I found myself feeling only admiration for Gordana, which isn't a hell of a lot of emotion.

"I am not in love with you," she said.

"I know."

"And you are not in love with me."

"No."

"That's good. That makes it simpler."

"How?"

"Do you think I am a little girl?"

"No."

"Amfred did until I taught him otherwise."

"Are you in love with him?" I said.

"With Amfred? With Ambassador Killingsworth?" She smiled mockingly. "He is married."

"That's no answer."

"He is old."

"He's fifty and he's rich."

"I like him. He is a foolish man, but I like him."

"Better than Arso Stepinac who's not so foolish and not so old and not nearly so rich?"

"Arso," she said. "He wanted to be engaged, but how could I be engaged to the Church and to him, too? But I agreed. It was to be a secret. He promised."

"Tell me about Killingsworth."

"Poor Amfred. He is so clumsy. But nice—like a big, clumsy, friendly dog."

"I assume that your grandfather doesn't know anything about either Killingsworth or Stepinac."

"Or St. Ives?" she said.

"Or St. Ives."

"Or a number of others," she said and stretched, thrusting herself against me. "You are very good." She giggled. "I cannot say in the bed so I will say on the floor. You are very good on the floor, Gospodin St. Ives."

"Why gospodin?" I said. "Why not comrade?"

"I am not a Communist," she said, "but, should the necessity arise—" She shrugged prettily. She did everything prettily and so far she was the prettiest liar I'd ever met.

"What happened to your engagement to Stepinac?"

"He became jealous. So I tore it off. Tore is not right, is it?"

"Broke," I said, suffering a bad case of déjà vu.

"Yes, I broke it off. He wrote me many letters. Passionate ones." She rolled her eyes naughtily. "One could not believe that a man who says he is of the police could be so passionate. There were so many letters that even Grandfather grew suspicious."

"Where is your grandfather?" I said. "Or have I asked that before?"

"He is detained," she said and closed her eyes and drew me down to her again, snuggling up against me.

"Where?" I said, propping myself back up on an elbow.

"Do you think I'm attractive?" she said.

"You know what I think."

"Would I be attractive in New York? Or Washington?"

"Anywhere."

She sighed deeply and snuggled some more. "It would have been so nice in New York, I think. Yes, I would prefer New

York. I am tired of living in a capital. Or perhaps I shall become a nun after all," she said.

"Isn't that the plan?"

She smiled, more to herself than to me. "That is the plan. My engagement to the Church. Such a long engagement. I could not wait." She pushed me away gently. "But now it doesn't matter."

"What doesn't?" I said.

"Nothing," she said. "Nothing matters because it's all over."

"What?" I could never recall asking so many questions and getting such nonsense answers.

"Come," she said, rising with a smooth grace and reaching for my hand, "let us go see Grandfather. He is waiting."

"Like this?"

"Come," she said, tugging me through a door and down a hall. "Grandfather is waiting." She was smiling now, but sadly, and some tears were rolling down her cheeks. I could only stare at her. "In here," she said. "He is in here."

She opened a door and Anton Pernik, Nobel laureate, lay quietly on a bed, his eyes closed, his hands clasped around a rosary. He was dead. She walked over to him, leaned down, and kissed him on the forehead. She turned to me, naked and lovely, and said, "He is dead."

"So I see. When?"

She looked around the room. All the religious artifacts and pictures that were missing from the sitting room had been hung on the walls of the bedroom. "He found comfort in such symbols," she said, making a vague gesture.

"When did he die?" I said, feeling more naked than I'd ever felt in my life.

"This morning. Early this morning. In his sleep. I don't think he minded. I don't think he really wanted to go to

146

America, but he thought I did. He thought I wanted to become a nun."

"Do you?"

I stood in the doorway without a stitch on, looking at the
lovely nude girl and her dead grandfather and, as if from a
distance, I watched my mind function. I wasn't proud of what
it did, but I was glad to see that it could still work. It did it
protestingly, sending out signals of distress and disgust, but
it kept on working and when it was done, it spewed out the
end product. It wasn't pretty.

"Do I what?" Gordana said.

"Do you really want to go to New York?"

She shook her head. "It is impossible now. I have no money.
My grandfather is dead. I cannot go."

"Do you want to?" I said. "Do you want to go badly?"

"Yes," she said softly. "Very badly. I'll do anything to go."

I stared at her, not liking her much just then, but not liking
myself at all.

"You may have to," I said.

CHAPTER 16

When I got back to the Metropol at seven o'clock I wasn't surprised to find Slobadan Bartak of the Ministry of Interior waiting for me in the lobby and looking as if he might spit acid.

He approached almost at a lope, his short torso thrust forward, his face screwed up into a twisted advertisement of anger and disapproval. I stopped and waited for him. He halted before me, locked his hands behind his back, teetered up on his toes, and when he spoke his voice was a bitter, petulant charge. "I have been waiting for more than an hour."

"Did we have an appointment?"

"You have heard from the kidnappers."

"Ah," I said.

"Well?"

"Let's make a deal."

"Deal?"

"A trade, a transaction."

148

"What kind of a transaction?"

"I'm sure that there's some old Yugoslav tradition that calls for a drink during negotiations."

"I know of no such tradition," Bartak said. "If one drinks, one drinks after negotiations, not during."

I took his elbow and turned him toward the bar and toward a drink I did not want. "Let's fly in the face of tradition," I said.

"Fly?"

"Where did you learn English?"

He stopped. "What is wrong with it?"

"Nothing," I said. "You speak it very well."

"I learned it at the government school," he said, once more moving toward the bar. "I was first in my class."

We chose a table in the corner and when the waiter came I ordered vodka. I was tired of plum brandy. Bartak ordered Scotch, probably because I was paying. Neither of us commented on the other's choice which was just as well because it only would have been something nasty.

Bartak tasted his drink and said, "You have heard from the kidnappers."

"You said that before."

"It is true."

I shrugged. "I may have."

"What do you mean may?"

"They only said they were the kidnappers."

Bartak wriggled forward in his chair. He was interested now. "What else did they say?"

"They were primarily concerned about the million dollars."

"Yes?"

"I told them that it was already on deposit for them in a

Swiss bank. The State Department made the arrangements, you know."

"When do they want to make the exchange?" Bartak said.

"It's as I said. They only claimed to be the kidnappers."

"What do you mean?"

"That they could have been anybody. My picture was all over the front page, the story was in all the papers. The call could have been a hoax."

Bartak pounced on that. "So it was a call?"

"Yes."

"But not to your phone in the hotel."

I wagged my head at him sorrowfully. "Now you've done it, Mr. Bartak. You've gone and tapped my telephone."

He looked as if he might try bluster at first, but changed his mind in favor of guile. His kind came equipped with a sly look. "Only as a precautionary measure."

"Of course," I said. "I understand your concern. But I'm still not sure that the call was from the kidnappers." It was only the forty-third lie that I'd told in the past few days and I wondered how long it would be before I no longer realized that I was lying.

"Why aren't you sure?" Bartak asked.

"Because I didn't talk to Ambassador Killingsworth. Unless I talk to him, there's no deal. No transaction. No exchange."

"You received a note," Bartak said in an almost accusatory tone.

"The note wasn't from Killingsworth."

"So," he said, drumming the fingers of his left hand on the table as if it helped him to think. "You are waiting to hear from Killingsworth himself?"

"Yes."

"When do you expect him to call?"

150

"They said tomorrow—late tomorrow."

"That is Saturday. That means that they will have had the ambassador for an entire week. That is too long."

"It's not unusual," I said. "At least not in the States. I worked one kidnapping case where they kept the victim for an entire month." I paused to finish my vodka. "Before they killed him."

Bartak looked up sharply. "Are you suggesting that they might kill the ambassador?"

"I suggested that the last time we met. Look at it from their angle. They've had Killingsworth for almost a week. He's heard them talk even if they've kept him blindfolded. He'll be able to recognize their voices, if nothing else. So once they get Pernik and the money, why shouldn't they kill him, especially if they think that the go-between has invited the police to hang around?"

"But surely you would not part with Pernik and the Swiss bank information until your ambassador is safe?"

I sighed. "Mr. Bartak, you have just hit upon the most delicate phase of the go-between business. It's who goes first, the go-between or the criminal? There is no foolproof plan, believe me, because I've desperately tried to dream one up. Now it's obvious that the kidnappers didn't expect me to bring along a million dollars in currency. So they accepted the promise that the U.S. government would deposit a million dollars in a numbered account. I've announced this to the press. But what if the numbered account doesn't exist? What recourse do the kidnappers have?"

"None," he said.

"Ah," I said, "but they do."

He looked puzzled for the first time since I'd met him. "I do not follow you, Mr. St. Ives."

"Look at it this way. The exchange has taken place. Mr. Killingsworth is back safe and sound in his embassy. The thieves have the Swiss account number. All they have to do is get to Switzerland and draw their money. But what, they think to themselves, what if the United States gave them a false number? Whom could they sue? Nobody. But they have one more thing to trade."

"What?" he said, completely absorbed with my tale.

"They have your Nobel poet, Anton Pernik. If the Swiss account turns out to be false, they threaten to kill Pernik—wherever he is—and dump his body in the middle of Trg Republike or Lafayette Park and then both Belgrade and Washington would have a hell of a lot of explaining to do. I think you'd rather spend a million dollars yourself than to have that happen, wouldn't you?"

Bartak shook his head, not in disagreement, but in seeming admiration. "You say there is no foolproof plan, Mr. St. Ives, but these Yugoslav kidnappers seem to have come up with one."

"It's not foolproof," I said, "because it's still based on faith. They believe that the U.S. government will deposit a million dollars to their account in a Swiss bank. Washington believes that they will hand over Killingsworth alive and well. Their ace in the hole—do you understand the expression?" He nodded that he did. "Their ace is Anton Pernik. My ace is my ability to cancel the Swiss account on a moment's notice. But the kidnappers are still risking their lives and they're betting that you won't blow the whole thing by barging in at the last moment. If that happens, I think I can promise you one thing: Killingsworth dies."

For a moment I thought I had him convinced. But he was a stubborn one. "I am not as stupid as you seem to think, Mr.

St. Ives. I have no intention of interfering with the negotiations to the point where Mr. Killingsworth's life would be endangered. His safety, as I've said before, is our paramount concern. But it is the only thing more important than the capture of the kidnappers. You said you had a proposition, a deal, you called it. I will now listen to it."

He folded his hands on the table, cocked his chin up in the air, and looked down his nose at me. He was all set to say No. I decided to hand him the surprise.

"Who do you think kidnapped Killingsworth?"

His nose came down an inch. "Do you mean their names?"

I shook my head. "I mean when the news first broke, who did you think it was? Somebody who was mad at you for keeping Anton Pernik under house arrest, some misguided patriots or poetry lovers perhaps?"

"We did suspect that," he said stiffly.

"But you now accept my theory that Pernik may be used as a kind of a hostage?"

He nodded. Reluctantly. "It has merit."

"The press would think so," I said and sat back to let it sink home.

His face got all scrunched up again to show that he was angry and when the full implications of what I'd said hit home he started turning a deep red, first his ears, then his neck, and finally his cheeks. When he finally spoke, it was a sputter. "That is blackmail!"

I nodded cheerfully. "I know. You might want to check it out with your own press people, but from my experience the headlines should go something like this: 'Yugoslavs Risk Nobel Poet's Life to Save U.S. Ambassador.' Of course, right now the press thinks like you did—that the kidnappers are friends or admirers of Pernik's."

The flush subsided in Bartak's face and when he spoke his tone was low and cold. And mean. "What is it that you want, Mr. St. Ives?"

"My deal, remember? You give me something, and then I give you something in exchange."

I waited, but he said nothing. He only stared at me and there was nothing in his eyes to indicate that he saw anything he liked.

I continued. "I want the guards taken off Anton Pernik's apartment within the hour. I want surveillance of me and my two colleagues ended immediately. You can keep the phone taps going because I won't say anything important anyhow." I looked at my watch. "I want thirty-six hours to get Ambassador Killingsworth back safely. If I fail to do so within that period of time, then I'll withdraw from the negotiations and recommend to the American embassy that they be handed over to you." Bartak brightened a little at that, but not much. He started to say something, but I waved him to silence.

"In addition, once Killingsworth is safe, I'll immediately furnish you with every detail that I have about the kidnappers. You can ask any kind of questions that you want and I'll volunteer every scrap of information that I think's pertinent. That's the proposition."

Bartak looked grim and about ten years older than he had when he first sat down at the table. I decided that the experience could only help his professional growth. "My counter proposal," he said, snapping it out. "I'll give you the thirty-six hours." He looked at his own watch. "Until five Sunday morning, correct?" I nodded. "I will not withdraw the guards from Pernik's apartment. The surveillance of you and your colleagues will have to be left to my discretion."

"Done," I said, but I didn't offer him my hand because I thought he might bite it.

He rose and teetered up on his toes again to give him more height. His face was a study in disdain, but I was almost accustomed to being looked at like that.

"I don't like to be blackmailed, Mr. St. Ives," he said and waited for a moment as if expecting a reply. When I said nothing he turned on his heel and marched out of the bar. I sat there, looking at my empty glass, and finally came up with a reply to his last remark. But it wasn't very clever and it wasn't even smart. It was only nasty and snide and I was glad that I hadn't come up with it sooner because I needed to list one good deed for the day and I couldn't think of any others.

CHAPTER **17**

When I came out of the bar the hotel's paging system started blaring my name through the lobby. At the information desk a rather uppity clerk sniffed and said that yes, there was a message for me, a note, but that "some person" had refused to leave it with the desk and was insisting on turning it over to me himself. The clerk pointed a nicely cared for finger at "some person" so I turned to see who it was.

He was no more than sixteen or seventeen and had pimples and wore his brown hair down around his shoulders in frizzy curls. He leaned against one of the walls, working hard on a mouthful of gum while he gave the Metropol's lobby and guests a contemptuous sneer. I walked over to him.

"Hi," he said.

"You got something for me?"

"You're Mr. St. Ives?"

"That's right."

"I got a letter for you. I'm supposed to wait while you read it." If his English had any accent, it was pure American and I suspected that he had learned it at the movies.

I waited for him to hand the letter over to me, but when he made no move, I said, "How much?"

His eyes were roving around the lobby again. "How much does it cost for a room here?"

"Mine costs two hundred dinars a day, but I held out for a view."

He whistled. "That's sixteen bucks."

"The letter," I said.

"I'm supposed to see some ID."

"Where'd you learn it?" I said, reaching for my billfold.

"What?"

"Your English."

He shrugged. "I belong to a film society."

"It must meet every day," I said and handed him my New York driver's license. He looked at it and then handed it back. One of his hands disappeared under the folds of his long green cape that looked as if it had been cut from a blanket and reappeared holding an envelope.

"I'm supposed to wait while you read it," he said.

"I know."

I opened the envelope and the message was brief, concise, even trenchant. It said:

> How do you propose to get a dead man out of the country? I think we should discuss it. The boy will guide you.
>
> Bjelo-Stepinac

"Shit," I said and put it away in my coat pocket.

The kid looked hopeful. "Bad news?"

"Just average," I said. "Let's go. What do we do, walk or take a cab?"

"I got my bike," he said. "You can ride on the back."

"Bike?"

"Motorcycle."

"We'll freeze."

He looked at me scornfully. "It's not that cold."

I glanced around the lobby. A man in a brown topcoat dropped his eyes back to his newspaper. A younger man suddenly became fascinated with a wall advertisement for JAT. I turned back to the kid. "Let's go," I said. "Right now."

He liked the idea and we moved quickly across the lobby, through the hotel's entrance, and out into the street. It was dark, but the streetlights furnished enough illumination to make out a motorcycle parked at the curb about a hundred feet away. The kid trotted toward it. I turned once to watch two men hurry from the hotel, buttoning their overcoats. They were the newspaper reader and the one who had liked the JAT poster.

The kid knew how to ride his bike. It was a 250 cc BMW and I never got around to asking him how long he had saved for it. He had the engine started by the time I got my leg over the buddy seat. He paused only long enough to give the throttle a couple of twists with his gloved hands to produce the standard varooms that are obligatory for all motorcycle departures and we were off. I twisted my head in time to see the two men who had been in the lobby pile into a Volkswagen. I shouted at the kid, "Can you lose a Volkswagen?"

He nodded vigorously and to prove it he made a sharp right turn off Bulevar Revolucije at the Federal Assembly which almost lost me instead. From there on he turned almost every block. We headed north and east, but after the first two turns I was lost. I gripped the back of the buddy seat at first, but that proved impractical so I held on to his waist. My hands froze there just as well. While they were freezing I kept thinking, "You're too old for this, St. Ives. Your bones are brittle with age." If he had stopped, I would have gotten off, but he didn't so I hung on and tried to think of someone to blame. I came up with Myron Greene and silently swore at him for a while and then tried to think of people who might know of a job in public relations.

The kid rounded another corner and screeched the machine to a halt. "What's the fare?" I said, getting off quickly.

He shrugged. "You don't owe me nothing."

I found a hundred dinars and handed them to him. "It was an unforgettable experience. Where am I supposed to go?"

"Down there toward the river," he said, pointing to a narrow street that sloped toward the Danube. He leaned forward to peer at me. "You know something?" he said.

"What?"

"That guy who gave me the letter."

"What about him?"

"He looks a lot like you. But he's younger."

"Everybody is," I said and turned, heading for the narrow street. The kid said good-bye with a couple of varooms that blasted off the buildings.

The street had no name that I could see, not even one written in the usual Cyrillic letters which make finding any place in Belgrade twice as much fun. The street was bordered by two large brick warehouses. I walked down it slowly, listening to the sound of my leather heels as they struck the pavement, making measured and solemn echoes.

There were no windows in the warehouses and the street that ran between them was barely wide enough to permit the passage of trucks. I noticed that in several places the bricks were scarred where drivers had misjudged either the width of their trucks or the narrowness of the street. I kept walking, listening to the sound of my footsteps. At the end of the street between two buildings was a darker patch of something that I took to be a slice of the Danube.

He came from the left, out of the setback in a warehouse. "Keep on walking," he said. It was Stepinac and he fell into step with me as we neared the end of the narrow street which really wasn't much more than an alley.

"I got your note," I said.

"The boy was the only messenger I could find," he said. "We need to talk."

"What about?"

"About Anton Pernik who's dead."

"I know," I said.

"It doesn't change your plans?"

"No," I said. "Not really."

"I do not like what you are doing to Gordana."

"I don't like it much myself."

"She said that you are going to take her to New York."

"Take isn't quite the right word," I said. "I'm going to try to see that she gets there."

"I have just come from her," he said.

"Oh."

"She made me promise not to report her grandfather's death."

I could have wondered how she made him promise that, but instead I said, "Your note said that you wanted to talk about Pernik."

"Yes."

"Well?"

"My superiors are not at all satisfied with the kidnapping."

"They don't like the technique?"

"The technique does not disturb them. The motive does."

"A million dollars adds up to a lot of motive," I said.

"Anton Pernik adds up to nothing."

"You'd better spell it out for me," I said.

"Very well. Just before your ambassador was kidnapped, I had spent many hours interviewing Anton Pernik about his past and present associations. A day would have been suf- ficient really, but I dragged the sessions out because of Gordana."

"Pernik told me about them," I said.

"Yes. Well, I came to know more about Anton Pernik than I really wanted to. Incidentally, he was a terrible poet. I also discovered two things. The first is that the American ambas- sador is in love with Anton Pernik's granddaughter."

"That doesn't seem to be much of a secret," I said. "The only ones who didn't seem to know about it were you and Pernik."

"I didn't quite tell you the truth in New York, Mr. St. Ives," Stepinac said. "One of the principal reasons that I spent so much time interviewing Pernik is because we were curious why the American ambassador should take such an interest in him."

"And you learned that he was interested in the grand- daughter instead."

Stepinac stopped and looked up and down the alley as if to make sure that no one was around. He needn't have both- ered. It was still deserted. "I also learned," he said, "that there is no one—no one in the entire world—who'd risk kid- napping a United States ambassador just to secure the release of that old man from house arrest."

"Maybe that wasn't their motive," I said.

"That's right. It wasn't their motive. It wasn't the poet that the kidnappers wanted, it was the granddaughter."

"There's another possibility," I said.

"What?"

"They may have wanted to use Pernik as a hostage, to make sure that the million dollars was paid." I'd just used the same theory on Bartak. I decided to see how it worked with Stepinac. It didn't go over.

"I might have accepted that theory yesterday, or even the day before," Stepinac said.

"But not now?"

"No."

"Why?"

"Because of your own peculiar actions, Mr. St. Ives. You have been under surveillance, you know."

"Yes."

"I think you are getting yourself into something which could prove most dangerous—and which really has nothing to do with either Pernik or his granddaughter."

"I'm not sure that I follow you."

"I thought that might be your reaction," Stepinac said. "That's why I decided to convince you."

"How?"

"I'll call it a direct confrontation," he said.

"With whom?"

We were at the end of the alleylike street. Stepinac stopped and looked at his watch. "We'll make our confrontation in exactly five minutes," he said.

"Where?"

He nodded across the street. "There." It was a small house, a cottage really, with mullioned windows that occupied a narrow lot between two buildings which looked like some more

162

warehouses. It was an anachronism snuggled in between two symbols of industrial progress and because of it, I had been able to catch my glimpse of the Danube. The cottage was snow-covered now and its lot seemed to run right down to the river's edge. At its rear I could see a small greenhouse and at the right of its front door was a fan-shaped trellis that might have borne climbing roses in the spring but was as bare now as the three large chestnut trees which grew in its small yard. A single light showed in one of the cottage's windows.

"Who lives there?" I said.

Stepinac looked at his watch again. "You'll know in five minutes."

We waited in the entrance of the alley, not talking, and when the five minutes were nearly up, Stepinac started across the street. I followed just as the lights of a car parked at the curb switched on. The car sped away from the curb quickly and I hesitated. Stepinac was already in the middle of the street. The whine of the engine shifted into a roar and Stepinac looked to his left. It may have been because he was tired, but he didn't move as fast as he had in New York, not nearly as fast, and the gray Mercedes smashed into him with its bumper and grill and slammed him flat on the pavement. It may have made a sound, but I couldn't hear it over the noise of the engine. The Mercedes didn't stop.

He wasn't dead when I got to him. His eyes were open, but I'm not sure that they saw anything. He muttered something, but I couldn't understand what it was. I put my ear close to his mouth and he seemed to mutter again and it sounded something like, "It was no accident this time," but perhaps that's only what I expected him to say. I'm still not sure. He had no other dying words, no revelations, no confession. Some blood came out of his mouth and ran down his chin. His mouth widened and for a moment I thought he was trying to smile, but he wasn't. He was dying instead and the stretched mouth was only a dead man's rictus.

I rose and crossed the street and knocked on the door of the cottage for a long time, but no one answered. I went back to the street and waited for a car to come by so that I could hail it, but none came. So I left him there in the street like that and walked up the alley and all the way back to the Metropol hotel.

CHAPTER 18

I waited until the debate about who sat where ended before I said anything and then I said, "You want to clear your throats? Maybe cough a few times?"

Wisdom looked at me from his seat by the window. "What's your trouble?" He turned toward Knight who was again sprawled on my bed. "Our leader seems to be under a strain. Have you noticed the tight lips, the nervous gestures?"

"He's probably decided to double-cross someone," Knight said. "He only wants us to reassure him that it's all in a good cause."

"The first plane out of here is at ten fifteen this evening," I said. "You'd both better catch it. The deal's gone sour."

Knight sat up and swung his feet to the floor. "God, St. Ives, when you get noble, you're really awful."

"I liked him better when he was a shit like us," Wisdom said. "I don't care much for him when he's Carstairs."

"Carstairs?" Knight said.

"Carstairs the magnificent. You know Carstairs. When they come to the edge of the desert he's the one who always turns to his two buddies and says, 'If you don't hear from me in three weeks, tell Mary . . .' Then he breaks off and god-damned near blushes and says, 'But you know what to tell her,' and then one of his buddies, the stupid one, like you, Knight, says, 'But that's fifteen hundred miles of burning sand, Carstairs,' and Carstairs, the prick, shades his eyes with his hand and says, 'Isn't that what all of life is?'"

Knight nodded several times. "Now I remember Carstairs. St. Ives does resemble him. The eyes especially."

"Shifty," Wisdom said.

"And the chin."

"Weak."

"And the mouth."

"Slack-lipped," Wisdom said.

"Why don't you tell us a little about it, Carstairs," Knight said, "and then we'll make up our own minds about what we'll do. Maybe we don't want to go back to New York via Frankfurt which is a lousy town anyway. Maybe we'll go to Venice."

"Or London," Wisdom said. "I know some girls in London. They'd be fascinated with my adventures in Belgrade—all about how I saw one real mosque and rented a car and got drunk once and then took a tour of the old Kalemegdan fort which is just a hell of a sight. I could tell them that I always have such madcap experiences when I go traveling with my old buddy Carstairs."

"All right," I said. "I'll tell you about it."

"Just don't go noble on us," Knight said.

"I only get those attacks once or twice a year," I said, and then told them about it—about Stepinac and who he said he was and how he got killed, about Jovan Tavro who needed to get out of the country, and about Anton Pernik who didn't because he was dead. When I was through they both thought about it for a few moments and then Knight was the first to ask a question.

"Who do you think killed the guy who looked like you?"

"I don't know," I said. "He was supposed to take me to see somebody or meet somebody, but we never made it."

"Any idea of who it was?" Wisdom said.

I shook my head. "None."

"So what do you want to do now?" Knight said.

"You know what he's going to do," Wisdom said and went over to the dresser and poured himself a shot of the plum brandy.

"I just want to see if he does," Knight said.

"He's going to substitute Jovan Tavro for the dead poet," Wisdom said and downed his drink in a gulp before turning to me. "Right?"

"All by yourself?" Knight said.

"Right," I said.

"Don't forget Gordana," Wisdom said.

"That's probably why he wants us to catch the plane."

"Look," I said, "this was supposed to be something simple. All you'd have to do is switch Gordana and her grandfather for the ambassador and then go on your way. Now it's something else. It could turn into something messy. I dragged you into it, so it's only fair that I should tell you why you'd be better off if you caught that plane."

Wisdom shook his head. "I liked him better when he was noble," he said. "He's really impossible when he's long suffering."

Knight lay back down on the bed and folded his arms un-

167

der his head. "What would you do if you were in our shoes, Phil?"

"Catch the plane," I said.

"Why'd you ask us to come?"

"I thought I might need some help."

"What do you think now that you really need it?"

"It's as I said. You can get into some bad trouble."

"Let me get a little mawkish for a minute," Knight said.

"You're very good when you're mawkish," Wisdom said.

Knight spoke to the ceiling. "How long have you known me and my wife?"

I shrugged. "Ten or twelve years."

"You'd say we're good friends?"

"Christ," I said, "don't start that what are friends for crap with me. This isn't one of Wisdom's practical jokes where somebody gets embarrassed, but nobody gets hurt. I don't know how it'll wind up, but somebody's already dead because of it. I don't want to be responsible for inviting anyone to go along to their own killing."

Wisdom went back to his chair. "If it's so tricky, why're you staying, Phil? The ambassador's no great pal of yours. From what you've told us, he's a shit. So why don't you just tell the State Department to find somebody else?"

"It's not that simple," I said.

"That's the part he hasn't told us," Knight said, moving his head to look at Wisdom.

"The dirty part," Wisdom said, "with all the girls."

"I tell you what, Phil," Knight said. "If you promise not to go noble on us again, I'll stay. I'll stay with the full knowledge that the entire deal is tricky and that I might get into mischief. I'm staying because I'm curious and because I think that you might need the help. Just don't go noble on us again."

"Me, too, Carstairs," Wisdom said. "No speeches, no declarations of friendship, no firm, manly handshakes. Just tell us what to do and we'll do it."

"Catch the plane," I said.

"No."

"All right," I said. "You're both now full partners in the Acme Go-Between Agency, Incorporated. And if I don't seem grateful, it's because right up until now I never knew what true friendship really meant and——"

"Now he's mushy," Wisdom said. "I liked him better when he was noble."

"And so," I said, "when you stub your toe, or the going gets a little difficult, such as when they're about to toss you out of the airplane, don't come to me and say, 'Phil, why didn't you tell us it was going to be like this?'"

"When do you pull the switch?" Knight said, pulling himself up to sit on the edge of the bed.

"Tonight," I said. "I meet Tavro at ten o'clock."

"Then what?"

"Then I meet you a block from Pernik's apartment."

"I think I know what you're going to ask next," Knight said.

"What?"

"Can I play a seventy-five-year-old man?"

It took me ten minutes to shake my tails this time, and I did it by switching taxis. I arrived at the Impossible Café and sat with a cup of coffee until 10:04 when Jovan Tavro arrived, looking more bitter and unhappy than I remembered. He sat down and a friendly waiter took his order for a cup of coffee.

"Jones got word to me that you wanted to meet," he said. "He did not say why."

"I didn't tell him why."

"So you can now tell me."

"We're going tonight," I said.

Tavro expressed his reaction by slowing the coffee cup on its trip from the saucer to his mouth. "So soon?" he said.

"So soon."

"I must make arrangements."

"You've already made them."

"But there are things that I need to prepare, to pack, to arrange for——"

"There's nothing," I said. "You carry what's on your back and in your pockets. That's all."

"But I have papers that are important."

"Were important," I said. "They aren't any more. You said you want out of Yugoslavia. Here's your chance. If you don't want to take it, that's fine with me."

Tavro took another sip of coffee while he seemed to debate whether to accept my invitation. His narrow face ducked once, then twice. I took it for a sign of agreement.

"Has this place got a back entrance?" I said.

He nodded. "It leads to an alley."

"Are you still under surveillance?"

He nodded again.

"How long before they'll notice anything?"

"Perhaps a quarter of an hour. Even more. I usually drop by here every evening."

"This late?"

"No, not this late, but it's not that unusual."

"All right," I said as I rose. "Let's go."

The Café Nemoguće was more crowded than it had been

during my last visit, the sign of an approaching weekend. Most of the customers were over thirty, possibly because the café offered no entertainment other than conversation, not even a jukebox. We brushed past waiters as we headed toward the rear of the café, but none of them seemed to pay us any attention.

Tavro turned to me. "We have to go through the kitchen," he said.

I nodded and motioned him to go ahead. He pushed through some swinging doors into the kitchen which was at least twenty degrees hotter than the café itself. Nobody even looked up as we went through another door and out into an alley.

"Now?" he said.

"Now we look for a cab."

We walked for fifteen minutes looking for one and all that Tavro did was grouse about there not being more time and worry about who would look after his roses. We finally caught a taxi in front of the Hotel Majestic on Obilicev Venac and I told Tavro to give the driver the directions.

The taxi was an old diesel Mercedes that chugged and gasped as it crept down the almost empty streets. The night had grown colder and the taxi's heater wasn't working and our breaths frosted against the windows.

"There should have been more time," Tavro said, his tone petulant, almost a whine.

"There wasn't any."

"Where do we go now?"

"We meet some people."

"People?"

"Persons."

"You did not say that there would be anyone else."

"No," I said, "I didn't."

"Who are they?"

"Friends."

"I do not like it. I should have been consulted."

"See whether the driver can go a little faster," I said.

Tavro spoke to the driver and the car sped up to twenty-three or twenty-four miles an hour. I looked back several times, but there seemed to be no one following. As we drove more deeply into the blocks of apartments and flats, the traffic became almost nonexistent. Belgrade is not known for its night life.

The driver said something over his shoulder to Tavro who replied briefly.

"What did he say?" I said.

"That we are almost there."

A new blue or black Mercedes sedan was parked at a corner and the taxi drew up behind it. I paid the driver and we got out. Wisdom left the driver's seat of the new Mercedes and walked back toward us. He held his hands out as if apologizing and when he got closer he said, "We couldn't help it, Phil. We tried but we honest to God couldn't help it."

"Help what?" I said.

The rear door of the new Mercedes opened.

"Help what?" I said again.

"Me," Arrie Tonzi said as she stood by the car's open door, smiling prettily at Jovan Tavro.

CHAPTER 19

The wind whipped around the corner, billowing out the long skirt of Arrie's brown suede coat. It picked up the strands of her blond hair and played with them for a moment before replacing them in a careless coiffure that she brushed out of her eyes with the gloved fingers of her left hand. The look she gave me was one of begging defiance, if there is such a thing. I glared at her and turned to Wisdom. "Get him in the car," I said, indicating Jovan Tavro who huddled into his dark overcoat. "The backseat."

"Who is the woman?" Tavro demanded.

"Just get in the car," I said and walked over to Arrie. I closed the door of the Mercedes, took her by the elbow, and led her unprotestingly to the shelter of an apartment building entrance.

"Wisdom says he couldn't help bringing you," I said. "Why not?"

She tried for her go to hell grin, but failed to managed it. "I threatened that I'd tell Lehmann."

173

"The embassy's press guy?"

She nodded.

"Tell him what?"

"That the exchange is on and that he can release it to the press."

I shook my head. "It took more than that."

She looked away and then looked back again. "I went up to your room and you weren't there. Henry and Park were, so I figured it out."

"Just like that?" I said.

"We got some new information today."

"Who's we?"

She made a small gesture. "My boss."

"What kind of information?"

"That something's gone wrong with the exchange."

"What?"

"That's all we got, Phil, I swear it."

"That still doesn't explain how you got Wisdom and Knight to bring you along."

She looked away again. "I told them that I'd learned something and that if I didn't get it to you, it would blow everything."

"They believed you?"

"I had to prove to them who I work for."

"Jesus," I said. "Okay. What else?"

"I don't know what my boss learned or heard, but he did hear something and he's having it checked out. It's about the kidnapping. If they find out what they suspect, they're going to move in whether State likes it or not."

"And that's your hot information?"

"I've got another item."

"What?"

"Somebody else is mixed up in the kidnapping."

"Who?"

She looked at me steadily this time. "Jovan Tavro," she said. "The man who's in the back of your car."

I took her by the elbow again and we moved back to the car. If the CIA were edging its way in, then Arrie Tonzi was its one link to me—unless she was lying about everything. Or they could have manufactured the story and then told her to peddle it around, just to see who'd buy. But if the CIA had somehow connected Jovan Tavro with the kidnapping, then they knew something that Hamilton Coors very much hadn't wanted them to know. No matter how I shook the puzzle, it refused to give a clear picture—except that I was stuck with Arrie Tonzi who, I decided, would have to earn her keep.

I knocked on the window of the Mercedes' front door. Henry Knight rolled it down. "You have what you need?" I said.

"Yes."

"Let's go," I said. "Park, you stay with our guest."

"I insist on being told what is happening," Tavro said from the backseat.

"What'll I tell him?" Wisdom said.

"A story."

"What about Arrie?" he asked.

"She goes with me and Knight. If we need any translating, she can tend to it."

Knight got out of the car. "You happy?" he said to Arrie.

"I'm here anyway," she said.

"Let's go," I said. We walked around the corner toward the building that contained the Pernik apartment. Through a glass door that led to the vestibule I could see two plainclothesmen seated in chairs. Both were nodding. I knocked on the door and one of the men stirred and looked around. I beckoned to him and he rose reluctantly. I turned to Arrie. "Tell him that we want to see Anton Pernik," I said.

She nodded. The man opened the door and Arrie began talking to him in Serbo-Croatian. He shook his head at first, but then I heard her mention Bartak's name and he began to look less surly. Finally, he held the door open and we went through.

"He wants to see our passports," she said.

Knight and I handed ours to her and she handed them to the plainclothesman along with her own. He glanced at them and then tucked them away in his pocket. He said something to Arrie and she turned to me.

"He says that he'll keep them until we come down," she said.

I shook my head. "Not all of us are coming down," I said. "Think of something to get them back."

She shook her head in bewilderment. "What?"

"You're the CIA agent, honey," Knight said, bowing slightly to the plainclothesman, "come up with something brilliant."

Arrie turned back to the plainclothesman and, holding out her hand, said something. The plainclothesman's eyebrows went up, he laughed and winked, and then brought out the passports and handed them to Arrie. She thanked him and then handed them to us.

"What did you tell him?" I said as we started up the stairs.

"That you and I might be spending the night and possibly wouldn't see him again before he went off duty."

"Well, if it wasn't brilliant, it was quick," I said.

Apparently, the two policemen downstairs were the only

ones on duty at night. None was guarding the door to the Pernik flat. I knocked and the door was opened immediately by Gordana Panić.

"Has anyone tried to see him?" I said.

She shook her head. "No one."

"What about Stepinac?" I said.

She ducked her head like a child caught in its first lie. "He came to see me, not my grandfather."

"But you told him that the old man was dead."

"I had to," she said. "It was the only way."

"Well, Stepinac's dead," I said, not trying to ease her shock, if there was to be any.

She repeated the word. "Dead?"

"Like your grandfather."

She gestured vaguely around the room. "But he was here and we talked and he had some brandy and—" She ended it there and looked at Arrie and then at Knight. "I don't understand," she said.

"I'll need some of his clothes," Knight said. "His overcoat and hat and gloves and a scarf, if he had one."

"Whose?" she said.

"Your grandfather's," I said. "Knight's going to impersonate him while we go past the guards downstairs."

"Pernik is dead?" Arrie said to me.

"That's right," I said.

"When did he——"

I interrupted her. "I haven't got time to give you a running explanation and you don't deserve one. Just pick up what you can as we go along."

"The clothes. I need his clothes," Knight was saying to Gordana.

"They're back here," she said, moving toward the bedroom

177

where the dead man lay. Knight followed her and I followed Knight. All three of us filed into the bedroom where the old man still lay clutching his rosary. "Good Christ," Knight said.

"In this cupboard," Gordana said, opening a closet.

Knight rummaged through it and took out a hat, a coat, and a scarf. "Did he have any gloves?" he said.

Gordana produced a pair from the drawer of a bureau and handed them to Knight. He put the hat on first, wearing it low over his eyes. He slipped into the topcoat which was too short for him until he stooped to compensate for its lack of length. He wrapped the scarf around his neck and most of his chin.

"Glasses," he said. "He wore glasses."

Gordana looked around the room. "I put them some place," she said. "Some place safe." She opened and closed drawers until she found them in what seemed to be her sewing box. "Here," she said, handing them to Knight.

"Is this your best mirror?" he said, pointing to the one above the bureau. She nodded and Knight took articles from the pocket of his own topcoat which he had folded on a chair. "That coat cost me two hundred and twenty-five bucks, skipper," he said to me. "It goes on the expense account if I have to leave it here."

"One double-breasted, foreign intrigue trenchcoat," I said. "Duly entered."

Knight removed Pernik's clothing and started opening his packages as Gordana and I watched. "All I could get hold of was powder and pancake makeup and an eyebrow pencil," he said. "But if it's only a quick glance, it may do."

"What about your hair?" I said.

"I'll have to shave off my sideburns," he said. "There's no time for dye and I couldn't find any in that hotel shop anyway. The hat and the scarf'll cover most of my hair. I can use powder in the eyebrows." He turned to Gordana. "Your grandfather have a razor?"

She nodded. "It is the old-fashioned kind with a straight blade."

"Don't you have one?" he said.

She shook her head. "I do not find use for one."

I could attest to that but I didn't. "Use the straightedge," I said.

"Where is it?" Knight asked.

"In the bath," she said. "Come, I'll show you."

While they were gone I stared at the old man who looked no deader than he had looked at half past five that afternoon when his nude granddaughter and her new lover had come calling.

Knight came back into the bedroom looking almost naked without his sideburns. Gordana followed him. "She watched," he said. "She likes to watch men shave."

"Cut yourself?" I said.

"Only a nick."

He turned to the mirror over the bureau and started applying the pancake makeup and the powder. "It's more a question of mimicry than it is of makeup," he said. "I just want to create an old man's face—any old man. But my movements— my walk and my gestures—will provide the real misdirection. If they recognize them as familiar, they won't look at the face too much. The familiar clothing will help too."

He worked on his face for fifteen minutes, rubbing here, patting there, and drawing lines with the eyebrow pencil. Then he put on the hat, an old, almost shapeless felt, and pulled it down low over his forehead. He wrapped the long, blue woolen scarf around his neck and chin, making it ride

179

high up on the back of his collar. He shrugged into the coat and adjusted the glasses so that they rode halfway down his nose. He looked up at the ceiling, as if trying to remember something, and then with a dip and shrug he started to walk across the room in a slow, shuffling, sliding gait that drew a gasp from Gordana.

"It is exactly how he walked!" she said.

Knight walked back toward us. "He walked on the outside of his feet," he said. "A lot of old men do." He peered at Gordana over his glasses, using a stooped, slouching posture. "How do you like it, my dear?" he asked in a deep voice that was an almost perfect replica of Pernik's—accent, inflection and all.

She glanced at her dead grandfather quickly. "You do not look as he looked, but you sound and walk as he did. It is fantastic."

"It'll be fantastic," Knight said, "if they ask me to say something in Serbo-Croatian." He slumped back into his old man's posture and shuffled out of the room. Gordana turned to me.

"I am—I am sorry about Stepinac," she said. "I did not mean to seem so stupid earlier, but it was a shock and I do not need any more shocks. I have had enough. How did he die?"

"It was an accident," I said.

She shook her head. "I did not love him, but he was nice to me. I am sorry that he is dead. That is not much, is it, to be only sorry?"

"You can't do anything else," I said. "Do you want anything here?" I gestured at the room and the bed where the old man lay.

She shook her head. "I want nothing from here. Nothing." She walked over and put her hand on her grandfather's forehead. "He is cold," she said and turned back to me. "Were we terrible this afternoon? If we were terrible, I will forget it."

"I don't know what we were," I said.

"I will forget only part of it then," she said. "I will forget only the terrible part. The rest I will remember. Will you?"

"I'll remember it all," I said.

She nodded, looked at her grandfather once more, and said something to him in Serbo-Croatian.

"What did you say?" I asked her.

She smiled faintly. "I said, 'Good-bye, Grandfather.'"

CHAPTER 20

The plainesclothesman who had looked at our passports wanted to talk. Arrie went first down the stairs followed by Gordana and Knight, moving slowly and carefully in his old man's gait. Arrie chattered away in Serbo-Croatian and when the guard looked up at Knight, Gordana moved in close to the policeman, smiling and murmuring something that caused him to look at her carefully.

As Knight went past the talkative guard, Gordana put her hand on the man's shoulder and he reached up and gave it a small squeeze. The other guard turned his attention toward his colleague's flirtation.

Knight moved slowly to the entrance door. Gordana caught up with him and took his arm, as a dutiful granddaughter should. Arrie and I followed and were almost at the door when the talkative guard called something. I couldn't understand what he said, but I did catch the name Pernik.

"What's he want?" I said to Arrie as Knight stopped and turned slowly. The guard approached him.

"He wants some papers that Bartak gave you for Pernik and Gordana," Arrie said. I stepped into the guard's path and made a show of taking the thick brown envelope from my pocket and handing it over. The man examined its contents and kept two forms. Arrie asked him what they were and he told her with a bored shrug. "They're the forms necessary for Pernik to leave his house," she said.

The plainclothesman handed me back the envelope, waved casually at Knight who gave him an old man's wave in return, and we left the apartment. I hurried to catch up with Knight. "Keep up your imitation," I told him. "Somebody might be watching this place." He nodded and shuffled on down the street until we were around the corner where the Mercedes was parked. I put Knight and Gordana in the backseat next to Tavro. Arrie sat between Wisdom and me in the front.

"Where to?" Wisdom said, starting the engine.

"I'll give you directions," I said.

As we started, Tavro said, "I demand to be told who these people are and what it is that you're planning, Mr. St. Ives."

I kept looking at a map of Belgrade as I said to Wisdom, "I thought you were going to tell him a story."

"I did," he said, "but he wasn't much interested. Which way?"

"The next left," I said.

"I repeat my request, Mr. St. Ives," Tavro said in a cold tone.

I turned partially in the seat. "The gentleman at the wheel and the one next to you are colleagues of mine. The young lady in the rear is your new granddaughter, Gordana Panić. The papers that I have which may get you out of the country say that you're Anton Pernik, a poet by trade."

Tavro muttered something. "What'd he say?" I asked Arrie.

"That Pernik is a discredited poet."

"He's also a dead one," I said.

"But his papers are still good?" Tavro asked, leaning forward.

"They're official, if that's what you mean."

"Did you kill him?"

"No," I said, "I didn't kill him."

"If you have his papers, it is a logical question," Tavro said. "Who is the other woman?"

"This one?" I said, turning to look at Arrie.

"Yes."

"She's with the CIA."

This time Tavro didn't mutter his comment, and I didn't ask for a translation. Profanity can be a universal language.

"You're telling everybody, aren't you?" Arrie said to me.

"I thought you could take the credit in case anything goes right."

"There doesn't seem to be much danger of that," Wisdom said. "By the way, where are we headed?"

"Someplace safe, I hope," I told him. "If I can find it again."

There wasn't much further conversation, especially after I got us lost twice. I kept checking the rear window for possible tails, but there seemed to be none. The night had grown much colder and it looked as if it might snow again. We spotted only an occasional pedestrian, bundled up against the cold and hurrying for home, as we threaded deeply into Belgrade's working-class residential district. It was nearly midnight before I found the narrow street that I was looking for. It looked almost deserted except for a dim light that burned in one house.

"We should not come here," Tavro said, looking around at the street.

184

"Stop at the corner," I told Wisdom. I turned in the seat to face Tavro. "Why not?" I said.

"It is not safe."

"It's safer than anyplace else I can think of," I said. "I don't know of any hotel that would check us in without a lifted eyebrow and a quick call to the police."

"I must protest it," Tavro said in the stubborn tone of a man not much accustomed to opposition. "It is far too dangerous."

"Whose house is it?" Knight asked.

"An American's," I said.

"Bill Jones?" Wisdom said.

"Yes."

"What's he got to do with us?"

"Nothing," I said. "We have to say out of sight from now until nine tomorrow night when we meet the kidnappers in Sarajevo. We haven't got anyplace to go and the cops are probably looking for us. They'll be looking for us in earnest when they discover that Pernik's dead and if we're unlucky, that won't be too long from now."

"What will you ask of Jones?" Tavro said.

"I'm not going to ask him to take us in," I said. "I'm just going to ask him if he knows where we can hole up until there's some traffic on the road to Sarajevo."

"He will not like it," Tavro said.

"You'd better come with me," I said. "Maybe you can encourage him to like it."

We got out of the car and approached Jones's house. His was the only light on in the street which was utterly quiet except for the sound of the wind. I knocked at the door. Jones opened it a scant four inches and peered out at me. He con-

185

tinued to look at me for several moments before he said, "What do you want, St. Ives?"

"Tavro's with me," I said. "We need to talk to you."

"It's late," he said.

"It won't take long."

He opened the door wide enough for us to enter and we followed him into the sitting room. He turned on a light. He wore pajamas and a dark gray dressing gown. On his feet were a pair of old slippers. "This isn't smart," he said.

"That is what I told him," Tavro said.

"We need a place to stay until early morning," I said.

Jones shook his head. "Not here."

"I don't mean here," I said. "There's six of us. We have to hole up."

"Six of you?" he said. "What the hell is it, a convention?"

"It is lack of planning," Tavro said and started to say something else until he caught my look.

Jones sank into the plum-colored chair and looked at the head of the wolf on the wall. "Remember when we got that wolf?" he said to Tavro.

"I remember."

"Nine years ago, wasn't it?"

"Nine or ten."

"I happened to be looking at it today."

"Why?" Tavro said.

"My wife wants me to move it out of the sitting room. So I was looking at it. Close. Guess what I found."

"I don't know."

"A bug." Jones reached into the pocket of his dressing gown and tossed something to Tavro who caught it and then dropped it. He picked it up and looked at it curiously.

"You removed it?" he asked.

186

"Sure I removed it. I was going to ask you about it when I saw you."

Tavro looked at it closely. "It is a new model," he said. "I am not familiar with it."

"When did you find it?" I said.

"This afternoon, right after I got through talking to you."

"It might not have been too wise to have removed it," Tavro said.

Jones looked at him and nodded. "There're a couple of other things that might not be too wise that I've wanted to talk to you about," he said. "Now that St. Ives is here, I know we'd better talk about them."

"What about some place that we can hole up?" I said.

Jones gave me a cold look. "You in a hurry?"

"I'm in a hurry," I said.

"If you'll listen a minute, you might not be in a hurry to go anywhere." He turned back to Tavro who, like me, was still standing. "What I want to talk about is—"

The woman's scream interrupted him. It came from the rear of the house. Jones was on his feet and moving fast toward a closed door when we heard the flat, sharp sound of a single shot. Jones jerked the door open and the tortoiseshell cat scampered into the room, its tail swollen double by fear and excitement. Two men followed the cat into the room. Both carried automatics. They were young and one had brown hair and brown eyes and a new-looking red scar on his left cheek. The other one was blond with blue eyes. The one with the scar on his cheek shot Jones twice through the chest. Then he turned the gun on me and I watched his finger with a kind of paralyzed fascination as he tried to make up his mind whether to pull the trigger. Instead, he looked at the blond with the blue eyes who had his automatic pointed at

Tavro. The blond man shook his head. They motioned us toward the corner near the tile stove. The brown-haired one knelt by Jones and went through the three pockets of the dead man's dressing gown. When he didn't find what he was looking for he shook his head at the blond man who snapped something at Tavro who held out his right hand, palm up. In it lay the bugging device. The blond man took it and put it away in a pocket.

They both backed toward the door that led to the rear of the house. The blond one went through first. The one with the brown hair hesitated, as if still trying to decide whether to shoot. After a moment, he decided not to and backed from the room, slamming the door after him. Neither Tavro nor I said anything until we heard another door close, far back in the house.

"They've gone," Tavro said.

"Who were they?"

"I don't know," he said.

"Do you know why?"

"No."

"I wonder if Jones did."

"The woman who screamed," Tavro said.

"His wife?"

"Probably."

"We'd better see," I said.

We went through the door that led from the sitting room and down a hall. The first room on the left was the kitchen. It had a door that led to a small yard that faced on an alley. The first room on the right was a bedroom. I went in followed by Tavro. Mrs. Jones, her gray hair spread over a pillow, lay in a large double bed, the covers down to her waist. She was naked except for the hole under her left breast. The two

188

tabby cats sat at the foot of the bed and stared at her with yellow eyes.

"Children?" I said.

Tavro shook his head. "They are away at school. The oldest boy is in America."

"What did Jones want to talk to you about?" I said.

Tavro turned his mouth down at the corners, making his face more fishlike than ever. "I do not know," he said.

"No idea?"

"I can only speculate," he said.

"Well?"

"It may have been about my attempt to leave the country."

"Why didn't he talk to you about it earlier?"

"You mean today?" Tavro said.

"Yes."

He turned from the dead woman. "I do not know."

"Why would they want the listening device?"

"I would assume that they are not only the killers, but also the listeners. The police would find the device overly interesting."

"I wonder if those two knew?" I said.

"Knew what?"

"What Jones wanted to talk to you about."

Tavro looked more gloomy than ever as he paused at the sitting room door that led to the street. "I haven't been thinking about that," he said. "I have been thinking of something else."

"What?"

"Those two who killed our friend Jones and his wife."

"Yes?"

"I've been wondering why they didn't kill us."

CHAPTER **21**

There are two roads to Sarajevo and after I was through telling them that Jones was dead, we took the shorter one which goes through Ub, Valjevo, Titovo Uzice, and Visegrad.

There wasn't much conversation as we left Belgrade. Arrie, sitting next to me, was silent for the most part, answering anything I said with monosyllables or just grunts when possible. Wisdom swore at the road and the Yugoslav bureau of public highways, if there was one. In the rear Gordana slept with her head on Knight's shoulder. Jovan Tavro stared out of the window, as if trying to memorize sights that he would never see again. It began to snow.

Traffic was light except for the trailer trucks, usually pulling tandems, that traveled in fast caravans as they headed for the town where only a little more than a century ago camels from Constantinople and beyond came down with bad colds because of the altitude. Sarajevo had been a major terminal on the caravan routes from the east. Now its chief fame rested on the assassination on St. Vitus Day in 1914 of an Austrian archduke and his morganatic wife by a teenager who got a lot of the blame for touching off World War I. If you took a long view of history, you could also blame Gavrilo Princip for World War II and any other conflict that's popped up since then—even, by stretching a point, for the one in Vietnam. It's something to think about and that's what I did as we drove through the snow that fell in wide, wet flakes, cutting visibility to less than thirty yards.

"The chauffeur that the archduke had took the wrong turn," I said. "Let's hope that you don't."

"What chauffeur?" Wisdom said.

"The one who was driving Franz Ferdinand and his wife, Sophie," I said. "In 1914."

"In Sarajevo," Wisdom said. "Bad security there. Worse than Dallas."

"Anyway, there had already been one attempt on his life in Sarajevo that day so they changed the route. But nobody told the car ahead of the one that the archduke was in so when it turned up a side street the man driving the archduke got confused and came to a dead stop until somebody straightened things out for him. He stopped right in front of Gavrilo Princip who had a revolver in his pocket. Princip shot Franz Ferdinand in the heart and when Sophie threw herself across her husband, she caught the second bullet. The Austrians took a dim view of all this and blamed the Serbs and so started World War I."

"What happened to Princip?"

"There was a law that nobody under twenty-one could be hanged in the Austrian empire. They tried him, convicted him, and threw him in jail. He died there."

"What happened to the chauffeur?" Wisdom said.

"I don't know."

By the time we passed Valjevo, the snow plows were out, trying to keep the road open. I switched places with Wisdom, cleaned off the rear window, and we started out again as the snow continued to fall, packed on the road now. Driving got tricky. I was dubious of going much over fifty kilometers an hour so we crept along, the Mercedes' lights revealing a lot of snow and an occasional road sign which said that the next town of any size was Titovo Uzice.

"What's Titovo Uzice like?" I said, twisting my head to look at Tavro.

"It's a place of much liveliness," he said, adding, "and little else. We had our first headquarters there in 1941, but the Germans drove us out. For every soldier they lost they killed as many as three hundred Serbian hostages."

"Any place we could stay?" I said. "We aren't going to make it much farther in this snow."

"I may know of such a place," Tavro said and I left it at that.

It was nearly three A.M. when we crept into Titovo Uzice and followed the highway markers to the town square that boasts a two-story-high statue of its namesake. That night it looked something like the abominable snowman. On Tavro's recommendation, we stopped at the Palace Hotel which was just across from the park. Taking Arrie along in case I needed an interpreter, I woke up the night clerk. He was in his thirties and willing to discuss our problem at length, but that still left him with just 120 beds and they were all full. Completely.

"Ask if he has any suggestions," I said.

"I already did. He said no."

192

As we turned to leave, the night clerk called us back. He looked apologetic and with much spreading of the hands and a number of elaborate, don't blame me shrugs he went into a long description. When he was through, Arrie turned to me and said, "He says that he has heard of a place that sometimes takes in travelers. He won't swear to its quality nor recommend its accommodations because he himself has never set foot in it, but he has heard that it exists."

"What is it," I said, "the local whorehouse?"

She asked him that and he looked shocked at first, then reddened, and finally shook his head vigorously. Arrie asked him another question and he answered her with a brief, prim sentence.

She turned to me. "I've got a general idea of how to get there," she said.

"How far?"

"About a mile."

It was less than a mile and it was off the highway on a side street where the snow was now about ten inches deep. When I stopped the Mercedes I had the feeling that we weren't going any farther that night even if we tried. It was a three-story building of gray stone that looked to be about fifty years old. It sat back from the street thirty feet or so surrounded by some tall trees that bowed beneath their frostings of snow. At one time the building might have been an elementary school or the headquarters for some regional government office. Even at night it had that grim look of utilitarian officialdom about it, but the modest green neon sign, written in Roman script, proclaimed it to be the Ritz Hotel.

"It's the town whorehouse," Wisdom said.

"The clerk at the Palace said no. We asked him."

"I do not remember it," Tavro said, "but I have not been here in several years."

"You want to go with us this time, Park?" I said and Wisdom said he would go anyplace if there were the chance of a bed. There was no bell so we banged on the door and after three or four minutes it was opened by a middle-aged man in a red wool bathrobe. He invited us in and hurried behind the registry desk where he took up his official position.

"*Deutsche?*" he said.

"*Nein,*" I said. "*Americanische.*"

"Very good," he said. "I can the English speak."

"There are six of us," I said, eyeing the keys in the rack behind the desk. Only four of the twenty-four of them seemed to be missing. "We would like rooms for the night and part of tomorrow."

"Six rooms?" he said. "That is many."

"Five will do nicely," I said. "My wife and I will share one, of course." I put my arm around Arrie and gave her a hug. She gave me a strange look.

"But six rooms available I have," he said. "It is the slow season."

"Five," I said firmly.

"If I said four, could I bunk in with Gordana?" Wisdom said.

"Five rooms," I said.

He started taking keys down from the rack. "If you will wait until I my clothes put on, I will with your luggage help," he said, getting all the verbs nicely tucked away at the ends of his phrase and sentence. Maybe he thought in Serbian, translated it into German, and then into English.

"That won't be necessary," I said. "My chauffeur here will see to it."

Wisdom touched two fingers of his right hand to his forehead and snapped, "Right away, sir, and shall I take the car for servicing?"

"That won't be necesary. Just see to the others."

"Yes, sir," he said.

"May I sign for myself and my guests?" I said.

"Of course," he said and slid the forms across to me.

"Our passports are in our luggage," I said, "but we'll send them down or show them to you in the morning."

He nodded and said that the morning would be just fine so I signed in Mr. and Mrs. Jeff Davis of Jackson, Mississippi, Mr. J. W. Booth, Washington, D.C., Mr. Wiley Post of Tulsa, Oklahoma, Miss Belle Starr of Winchester, Virginia, and for Tavro, I signed Lou Adamic, Hollywood, California. I also insisted on paying in advance.

When Wisdom came back with the rest of our carload, but without any luggage, he got a strange look from the proprietor. I told him that my chauffeur informed me that the trunk was frozen and that we would have to wait until morning to open it, but in the meantime we were anxious to be shown to our rooms. I also told each of them the names I'd used to sign us in.

Arrie and I were the last to be shown to our room and I suddenly remembered that I hadn't eaten since lunch and that I was starving. I asked the proprietor if there were any kind of food available and he said that there was some *alaška čorba* left over from dinner and that he would even join me in a bowl. He invited us to meet him in the dining room.

"What's *alaška čorba?*"

"Fish soup," Arrie said. "Yesterday was Friday."

Our room was just a room with a bed, a couple of chairs, a table, and sink with no stopper. Arrie fished in her purse and brought out a large cork. "Here," she said, "I'm never without it. I've also got one toothbrush which I'll share with you, if you don't mind my dirty mouth."

"I haven't so far," I said.

She took off her coat and put it on a hook. There was no closet. "Who was Bill Jones?" she said.

"One of yours supposedly."

"What do you mean?"

"He said he was a sleeper, but if he told me that, he had a loose mouth, although he didn't seem the kind who would. You never heard of him?"

"Never."

"He came back in forty-eight after the war and lived here ever since."

"That took some doing in forty-eight if what I've heard is right," she said.

"That's what he said. He knew Tavro and Tavro apparently squared it with his boss."

"Alexander Rankovic?"

"The same. Jones fought with the Partisans."

"Huh."

"What's that mean?"

"It just means huh," she said. "If I remember my crash course in Yugoslav history, there weren't many Americans fighting with Tito. The U.S. liked Mihailović and his Cetniks better."

"So did the British," I said.

"At first," she said. "Then they switched to Tito and parachuted Randolph Churchill in to show that they meant business."

"Jones said he was a radio operator with OSS."

"He could have been, but there weren't many of them."

"You don't think he was."

She shrugged. "What does it matter now?" she said. "He's still dead."

We joined our host in a small dining room. There was bread and wine and the *alaška čorba* which turned out to be something like a Slavinized bouillabaisse with lots of paprika which I found quite tasty.

"You are my first American guests," our host said. "An honor you are doing us."

"Not at four o'clock in the morning," I said.

"It is the slow season. Next spring and summer will be many Americans coming."

"Did they last summer?"

He shook his head. "Last summer we were not open. It was still the time that I must the permissions get."

"What permissions?" I said.

He spooned some more of the stew into his wide mouth, wiped it with the sleeve of his bathrobe, and tore off a dou-ble-fistful of bread. He dunked the bread into the stew and crammed about a third of it into his mouth. As he chewed he studied us with a pair of pale gray eyes, the kind that you somehow expect to be blue and are faintly pleased and sur-prised when they aren't. He seemed to be calculating how much of his story we were interested in and whether his Eng-lish was up to the effort.

"Since The Reform," he said, "I must the permission get to open my hotel. It is private enterprise, yes?" I nodded. "So it is also a political question. First, the Communal Committee must its order of appearance decide—when to place it on the—" He stopped and said a Serbo-Croatian word to Arrie and she replied, "agenda."

"Yes, agenda," he said. "Then the local organization of the Party must be consulted and then the veterans and the Socialist Union and the Socialist Youth and the Socialist Alliance of Working People. All must have their say, for serious questions must be answered."

"What kind of questions?" Arrie said.

"Such as whether I can employ five workers or three. That is very important. Secondly, and I must to my own language go back for this." He rattled off something that Arrie translated as, "Whether the Ritz Hotel, under the conditions of a socialist economy, will lead to a capitalist relationship or be completely integrated into the socialist system."

"What did they decide?" I said.

"If I only four workers employed, there would no danger to our system be. So, I have four workers." His eyes twinkled. "But also I have my wife, myself, my three sons, and their wives. They are family and do not count."

I told him that his competition up the street at the Palace Hotel was not at all eager to admit that the Ritz existed. He snorted. "Of course not," he said. "They are afraid that I will away from them the tourist trade take. That is one. Two, they are all Serbs there and I am a Bosnian." He paused. "That makes a great difference. But soon I will have an answer to my petition. Already through the Communal Committee it has gone."

"What petition?"

"By spring I will two large advertising boards have at the ends of the city. They will draw much trade from the roads. It will in three languages be."

"Where'd you get the name?" I said, finishing the last of my soup.

"You do not like it?" he said.

"I think it's fine. Ritz Hotel. Nothing wrong with that."

"There was much debate," he said. "I wanted to call it the Hotel Uzice. I lost."

"Who wanted Ritz, your wife?"

"No," he said, "the chairman of the Socialist Alliance of Working People."

CHAPTER 22

I didn't awake until nearly ten when the management of the Ritz Hotel sent a smiling daughter-in-law up to our room with coffee. Arrie was still in bed, her mop of blond hair barely visible above the covers. She peeked out at me with one eye.

"Who the Christ was that?" she said.

"Room service with coffee."

"What time did we get to sleep?"

"I don't know; around five."

"Screwing's the best tranquilizer there is."

"They've been trying to package it in one way or another for years."

She propped herself up in bed and I handed her a cup of coffee. "Takes two though," she said.

"Or three."

"You like that?" she said.

"What?"

"Threesies and foursies and whole rooms full, I guess."

"Three is better than one, but two is better than three."

"You're conventional."

"Backward," I said.

"Hey, we tried that too last night, didn't we? I like that."
She was sitting up in bed now, her knees up to her chin.
"I'm going to have to try the other some time."

"What?"

"A threesome. You want to play?"

"Sure."

"You'd want another girl, wouldn't you?"

"I'm selfish."

"Who?" she said.

"Who what?"

"Who'd you want?"

"I'll let you send the invitation."

"How about Gordana?"

"That's a possibility."

"Huh."

"Huh what?"

"I was just thinking," she said. "About Gordana. She
wouldn't be bad at all, would she?"

"Not bad," I agreed.

"I never thought about it before. I mean not just like that,
not imagining one particular person. What do you think she'd
say?"

"Yes or no," I said.

"How do you ask someone? I mean do you just say, 'How'd
you like to join us in bed tonight because we think you're
pretty sexy looking?' "

"That's one way."

"What's she going to do now that her grandfather is dead?"

"I don't know," I said.

"Is she still going to become a nun?"

"I think that's postponed."

"But she wants to go to the States?"

"Yes."

"That shouldn't be any problem for her now. Passports aren't hard to get. Why doesn't she just get one and go? Why does she have to go through all this kidnapping exchange thing? They aren't after her."

"I'm trying to get the ambassador back, remember?" I said. "They're expecting Gordana."

"What about Tavro?"

"If he's lucky, he can use her grandfather's exit permit to get out of the country. Permits aren't easy for people like him to come by."

"How'd you get mixed up with Tavro?" she said.

"Just curious?"

She shook her head. "My boss can't figure out how he got involved in the kidnapping. Tavro was very bad news at one time."

"When?"

"When The Reform started. You know what The Reform is?"

"The decentralization of power, both political and economic," I said, droning the words. "It's been going on for years."

"Tavro was one of those old timers who tried to stop it. He got bounced for his trouble. Now there're others who think it's gone too far. My boss heard that Tavro is peddling information."

"What kind?"

"The kind that can get him in trouble."

"Maybe that's why he wants to leave the country," I said. "You don't talk much in the morning, do you?"

"Get dressed," I said. "I'll meet you downstairs."

"Shit," she said and kicked back the covers.

"At the end of the hall," I said. "Last door on your left."

Gordana, Knight, and Wisdom were in the dining room having breakfast. I joined them and asked where Tavro was.

"He went out," Wisdom said. "About thirty minutes ago."

"For what?"

"To buy a razor," he said. "I told him to buy four of them."

"Did you have a nice sleep?" Gordana asked me.

"Yes, thank you."

"Miss Tonzi did not keep you awake?"

"Not so that I noticed."

"That is very good," she said and smiled sweetly while Knight and Wisdom followed the conversation with deepening interest. "I was worried that you would not get enough sleep."

"Nobody worried about how much I got," Knight said.

"I did," Wisdom said. "I worried so much I couldn't sleep myself." He turned to Gordana. "I even thought of coming by your room so that you could worry about St. Ives and I could worry about Knight."

She smiled at him. It was a lovely smile and Wisdom basked in it. "You should have," she said. "Perhaps we could have comforted each other in some fashion." She patted him on the cheek and he smiled and I sipped the coffee that one of management's daughters-in-law had brought.

"Maybe we could console each other tonight," Wisdom said.

"I am not sure where we will be tonight," Gordana said.

203

"Mr. St. Ives has not told us." She smiled again at Wisdom. "But it is an interesting thought."

"With luck, you'll be in either Venice or Vienna," I said.

"And with no luck where will we be?" she said.

"I have no idea."

"When do we start?" Knight asked.

"As soon as Tavro comes back."

He came into the dining room then, bundled up in his dark overcoat, his carplike face pink with cold. He beckoned me to join him and Wisdom said, "Make sure he got some blades."

Tavro drew me out into the lobby and then looked around carefully. "I have been making inquiries," he said.

"About what?"

"Transport."

"You mean trains and buses?"

He nodded. "They are being watched."

"Looking for you?"

"I am not sure," he said. "There has been a murder."

"Jones?"

He shook his head this time. "The radio," he said.

"What about it?"

"It identified the murdered man."

"Who was he?"

"The news report that I heard said that it was an American."

"Not Jones though?"

"No. It said that the man was Philip St. Ives."

The dead man had to be my look-alike, Arso Stepinac. I tried to digest the report of my death, but it wasn't much use, so I asked Tavro, "Who identified the body?"

"Someone from the American embassy. Its press attaché, I think. I do not remember if they gave his name."

"Lehmann," I said. I kept on trying to think, to sort it all out, and I thought I was almost getting somewhere when Tavro said, "How will this affect your plans?"

"How the hell should I know?" I said.

"That is why I was making inquiries about transport."

"You'd better stick with us," I said.

His normally glum look changed into one of despondency. "I apparently have little choice."

"Did you buy the razors?" I said.

He nodded and produced four plastic-handled safety razors from his pocket. "They come with blades," he said.

"Give me one and tell the others to shave and get ready. We're going to leave within the next twenty minutes."

Arrie was pulling on her pantyhose when I entered the room.

"Any hot water?" I said.

"You'll have to use the cork."

I ran some water into the basin and used a thin bar of soap on my face. While I stroked off the whiskers, I said, "You said your boss was thinking of moving in on the kidnapping. Your real CIA-type boss, I mean."

"That's what I said."

"You never mentioned his name."

"No," she said. "I didn't."

"Why?"

"I didn't think it was any of your business."

I cut myself, just below the earlobe where it bleeds forever. I swore and Arrie came over to the basin. "Here," she said and patted a piece of Kleenex over the cut. I sliced off another swath of whiskers. She watched me.

"What's your boss's name?" I said, working now on the ones that grow just below the nose.

"It's still none of your business."

"I can guess."

"Go ahead."

"Gordon Lehmann, the insecure press attaché."

She laughed. "Gordon! He's a fuckhead."

"But he's your boss."

"You're nuts."

"Don't press it so hard," I said. "You said your boss was moving in on the kidnapping. Well, Gordon Lehmann sure as hell moved last night."

"How?" she said.

I rinsed out the razor and handed it to her. "Put it in your purse."

"How?" she said again.

"Gordon Lehmann identified my dead body."

She bit her lower lip and squeezed her eyes closed as if trying to think. Then she opened them wide. "I told you he's a fuckhead."

"He's also CIA."

She sighed. "Yes," she said, "the fuckhead's also CIA."

Maybe it was because it was Saturday, but except for the new buildings around its main square, which imposed a measure of decorum, Titovo Uzice reminded me of some brawling, wide open western town where the nearest law is over in the next county and likely to stay there.

We were looking for a gasoline station and the main street was jammed with men who reeled in and out of tiny grog shops. Women in a bastardization of native dress lined up at shops accompanied, often as not, by a squealing pig and a squawling child. Arrie, Wisdom, and I wandered into one dim place that featured four bearded cutthroats seated at a rough table, hacking away at lumps of meat and chunks of bread with their eight-inch pocket knives, and no doubt plotting the city's next crime wave. When they learned that we were Americans instead of Germans, they ordered a round of drinks. I couldn't identify what it was, but it burned all the way down and in revenge I bought a double round for them. The filling station, they said, was near the market, across the square, and around a corner.

We threaded our way through the sidewalk drunks and then fought the car through the human traffic. The men were taller than most Yugoslavs, but the women seemed dumpier. Nearly everyone pulled, carried, or wore some kind of livestock—pigs, chickens, or lambs which they draped around their necks. The market stalls, another bastion of free enterprise, offered on-the-job training in bitter haggling and a refresher course in sharp dealing, its practices and methods. Horses, sometimes hitched to high-wheeled carts, added to the general merriment.

"It hasn't changed a great deal," Tavro said. "It is still very much like it was before the war."

"The snow didn't seem to bother them," I said.

"Some who live thirty kilometers away were up at three or four o'clock so that they could make it to market," he said. "It is the custom."

Wisdom drove into the new-looking eight-pump gasoline station which offered something called Jugopetrol. While we waited for the attendant to fill the Mercedes' tank I switched on the radio and caught what seemed to be a news program. Arrie gave a running translation and her voice cracked a little when she said, "The man was identified by the press

attaché of the American embassy as being Philip St. Ives of
New York City. Authorities are conducting a wide search for
the driver of the hit-and-run automobile."

"You're dead," Knight said.

"I know."

"How does it feel?"

"Premature."

CHAPTER **23**

The news of my death provided a conversational topic all the way to Visegrad where we crossed the Drina River over the bridge about which they've sung songs, recited epics, and even written a novel. The trip through the Zlatibor Mountains down to the valley of the Drina had been a series of memorable skids, fine views, and outstanding profanities by Wisdom who fought the Mercedes through the icy hairpins and switchbacks of the road that turned and twisted back upon itself like a piece of wet string. The view of Bosnia to the north and Montenegro to the south was spectacular in spots, awesome in others.

"We fought through here," Tavro said in a somber tone and I decided that he was essentially a man without humor. "It is a harsh land."

The bridge at Visegrad with its four and a half arches on one side and five and a half on the other rested on massive pillars built of stone which was the color of honey and we slowed down at its center, like a carload of Kansas tourists, to read the inscription which according to Arrie's rapid translation said, "Bridge built by Mehmed Pasa Sikolovic in 1571. Destroyed or damaged by Germans in 1943 and rebuilt between 1949 and 1952. And that makes it four hundred years old."

"You're in Carstairs country again, Park," Knight said.

"How so?"

"We've just left Serbia and we're now in the state of Bosnia-Herzegovina."

"Ah," Wisdom said. "The Gothic Carstairs."

"Absolutely."

"This," Wisdom said, "is where Carstairs always flings his long, black cloak over his lean frame, thrusts the brace of finely wrought pistols through his belt, and plunges out into the bitter Herzegovinian night, his footsteps echoing hollowly on the worn steps of the ancient castle."

Sarajevo lies halfway between Trieste and Istanbul although it's difficult to get there from either place. We arrived just before dusk, having averaged a nifty thirty-two kilometers an hour since leaving Titovo Uzice at eleven. We came down through the narrow gorge that leads into the city which stretches along the banks of the Miljacka River just in time to glimpse a minaret or two.

"Which way?" Park said.

"Drive around," I said, "we haven't got anything better to do until nine."

We drove around for half an hour, slowing down for a look at the fairly new bus station and the Mosque of Gazi Husref Bey which Tavro said was the finest in Sarajevo. It had a flattened dome that sat on an octagonal drum which rested on a square mass. I preferred the Bascarsija Mosque near the market better with its minaret that shot up toward the sky.

"I like minarets," Wisdom said. "It's like they're always giving somebody the finger."

"When you find a place to park this thing," I said, "we'll leave it."

Wisdom found a spot about a block from the mosque and backed the car into it. "What do I do with the keys?" he said.

"Mail them."

"Putnik's going to be a little upset."

"Did you give them a deposit?"

"No."

"Then they'll be happy to get them back."

"I am very hungry," Gordana said. "Also I must go to the toilet."

"Knight, do you want to be tour leader?" I said.

"You're doing fine," he said. "I've got some film here that I'd like to get developed."

"And I'm hungry, too," Arrie said.

"It isn't going just quite the way I expected it to go, ladies and gentlemen, but if you'll bear with me for a while, I'll try to see to it that your bladders are emptied and your stomachs are filled."

It was dark now, but the streetlights were on here and there, which gave some illumination to the narrow lanes of the old section called Bascarsija that I herded my charges through like a mean shepherd with five ewes that were about to lamb. If I'd wanted to buy a copper Turkish coffee pot, I could have struck several magnificent bargains. The rug

211

merchants were out in force and there were places to have your fez ironed. Some of the men were down from the hills with their heads wrapped in red and striped turbans. A few wore braided belts and gusseted britches under their long sheepskin-lined coats. Others wore suits that looked as if they came from the state cooperative store while still others, a sinister lot, I thought, wandered about in blue, chalk-striped double-breasted suits that could have been new in 1930 or 1970.

The women seemed to wear anything that came along although Arrie's long suede coat got a couple of admiring glances. With the veil still banished, the Muslim women drew their kerchiefs across their mouths. Some wore what looked to be pants suits, but weren't, and others of the Muslim faith wore bloomers to make sure, the story had it, that no baby who just might be a descendant of the Prophet would touch soil at his birth.

It was a noisy section, flavored by the Orient as well as the West, and nobody seemed to be much concerned with The Reform. They were there to do business with anyone who came by and if it took six cups of coffee to make a deal, that too was Allah's will.

We turned left at a narrow street that had no name, then right on to Asćiluk, and then left to the main road, Vojvode Stepe Obala.

"It is the bridge across the way that is named for the hero, Gavrilo Princip," Tavro said mournfully.

"Is that where he shot the archduke?" Wisdom said.

"No," Tavro said, "it is near here where we stand."

"What about a café or a restaurant?" I said.

"There is one called the Dva Ribara," he said. "It is not far."

"Let's try it," I said. It seemed to be the first real decision that I'd made all day.

It wasn't much of a restaurant, but it offered food, and Henry Knight and I, alone at the table, studied the menus as best we could. Knight folded his and put it down.

"I'll let someone else order for me," he said.

"What about a drink?"

"I can order that myself."

We tried the plum brandy again. Knight fooled with the stem of his glass, moving it in small loops around the table. "Have you come up with any conclusions?" he said.

"About the radio story?"

"Yes."

"None."

"What about the kidnappers?" he said.

"You mean will it have scared them off?"

"That occurred to me."

"And me. It was probably meant to."

"Could that embassy guy have made a mistake?"

"You mean an honest one?" I said.

"Any kind."

"It depends on what kind of shape the body was in. Stepinac did resemble me and there could have been some problem about identification. But I don't think that there was."

"But you can't guess why?"

"I can guess," I said.

"So can I," he said.

"What's yours?"

"It's not a guess really. It's just that somebody wants you dead for a little while. So it's really not guessing about why but about who."

"I can think of several who's," I said.

"Anybody I know?" Knight said.

"I'm not sure."

The table talk was less than brilliant. Tavro appeared to have sunk into one of his despondent moods and spoke only when someone asked him a question, and that wasn't often. Gordana, still looking lovely, seemed to have lost her appetite, but it may have been the food which she pushed politely back and forth across her plate. Arrie appeared thoughtful. She ate her meal quickly and then sat back, silently smoking a cigarette. Wisdom was still driving the car and his movements were tense and his speech was nervous chatter to which no one much listened, not even himself. Knight was the most relaxed, but then he was an actor and I couldn't tell how he really felt. I felt rotten.

The meal dragged on, prolonged by the indifference of the waiters who showed up at odd times, looking as if they'd rather debate management policy than serve the coffee. The restaurant filled up slowly and I called for the check at a quarter after eight and it arrived at eight thirty which I thought was reasonable haste. I showed my appreciation with a ten percent tip.

We crossed the river near Sarajevo's municipal museum and started through the Gypsy quarter of Dajanil Osmanbeg. It was a steep winding street, almost too narrow for a car. Small, evil-looking alleys led from the street and seemed to disappear into nothing.

"There is another way," Tavro said, "but this is quicker."

"So is a taxi," I said.

We followed him through the street that wound through Bistrik which might have been a suburb of Sarajevo at one time, but now was a collection of shacks and wooden houses that tilted crazily at each other. It was a Muslim district with a sprinkling of miniature mosques and minarets built of wood. The Gypsies were short and swarthy, as most Gypsies are, and they talked to each other in what Arrie claimed to be Tamil. Kids were everywhere, but they were outnumbered by the cats, lean, tough, Gypsy-looking cats that prowled the alleys or sat in doorways and stared up at us with the knowing eyes that a Gypsy cat would have.

"The Prophet was terribly keen on cats, you know," Wisdom said as we stumbled over a couple of kittens who pranced around spitting fiercely and arching their backs and puffing up their tails only to forget what they were mad about in the next second.

"I didn't," I said.

"You can see the mark of His hand on their heads," Wisdom went on.

"Truly," I said.

"There is a legend."

"Ah."

"Mohammed cut off a piece of his robe rather than disturb the cat who was sleeping on it."

"There must have been an easier way," I said.

"Then there would have been no legend."

I looked back several times, but if we were being followed, I couldn't spot the tail in the dim streets. If there were more than one, they could have been ducking in and out of a score of dark alleys and doorways. I didn't feel as if I were being followed, but then I never did which must indicate a low level of paranoia if nothing else.

"Left at the next street," Tavro said and we turned out of the quarter and onto a wider thoroughfare that commemorated the Sixth Day of November which, Tavro informed me, was a state holiday whose occasion he couldn't recall. It was his only failure as a guide thus far and I think it upset him a little.

"The train station is left at the next corner," he said and I turned to inspect the group which I reluctantly was beginning to think of as a brood. Wisdom was with Gordana and Knight was with Arrie.

"This is a dead-end street," I said. "The train station is about a block up. This time I'll go by myself. If I'm not back in ten minutes, I suggest that you check in with Traveler's Aid."

"It's cold here," Arrie said.

"Thank you for your cooperation," I said, turned and walked toward the station. I looked back twice at the five of them who huddled at the corner in a disconsolate group, looking something like a Salvation Army band that had lost its instruments.

The station was nearly empty except for a couple of Gypsies who were more interested in the tile stove than the next train and a shaggy-haired man in his thirties who wore a long, sheepskin-lined shepherd's coat, a fur hat, and scuffed leather boots. He looked at me and I looked at him. Then I looked at my watch and wandered over to examine the train schedule.

"You figure on catching a train?" a voice said and I turned. It was the shaggy-haired man.

"I hadn't thought of it," I said. He needed a shave and maybe a bath, but he probably knew it as well as I did.

"The radio said you were dead. Hit-and-run."

"Then what're you doing here?"

"We took a chance."

"How's Killingsworth?"

"You ever spend a week with him?"

"No."

"Don't," he said and looked around the station carefully. "You weren't followed?"

"None that I could spot."

He was a little shorter than I with dark brown eyes and quick, nervous movements. His hands made rapid, fluent gestures.

"You're the Italian," I said.

He nodded. "My partner's staying with Killingsworth. Where're the rest of them?"

"At the corner."

"How many?"

"Five. Two women, three men."

He rolled his eyes a little at that, but then gave me a magnificent shrug which made it perfectly clear that he considered them to be my foolish responsibility and one which would rest lightly on his shoulders for only a brief time.

"I got a Volks bus outside," he said. "We may as well go."

I followed him outside to a three- or four-year-old gray Volkswagen microbus that had chains on its rear wheels. I looked around again, but I could still see no one other than the two gypsies in the train station. The Italian also took his time before climbing up into the driver's seat.

"You sure you weren't followed?" he said, starting the engine.

"Hell no, I'm not sure."

"Cool it, friend, we're almost home." He paused a moment and then gruffly asked, "What do you think of my English?"

"It's swell."

"That's what he says."

"Who?"

"Killingsworth."

"What's he been doing?" I said.

"Chopping wood and when he's not doing that, he talks. He says he's going to write a story about us."

"What do you tell him?"

"That we're going to kill him. It keeps him quiet for a little while."

"He still thinks it's for real?"

"All the way," the Italian said.

"What's the schedule?"

"I'll get you up to the castle. Then you're on your own. Okay?"

"Okay," I said.

"Okay."

He pulled the Volkswagen up to the corner and I got out. The two women got in first, then Wisdom and Knight. Tavro seemed to hesitate. "What's the matter?" I said.

"I must know your plan," he said.

"Get in," I said, "and I'll try to think of one."

CHAPTER 24

We went south along the highway that climbs back
into the mountains. About ten miles out of Sarajevo we
turned east onto a narrow road which the snowplows had
given only a lick and a promise. The Italian had to keep the
Volks bus in first or second gear most of the time because it
was a steep, twisting road with sharp, unannounced cutbacks
and nearly right-angled corners. On the right I could see the
side of a mountain, on the left I could see nothing—no guard-
rails, no billboards, only the edge of the road that I was sure
dropped straight down for at least half a mile.

The Italian drove with all the fine, unconcerned flair of his
race. I was glad that we were going up instead of down because the grade kept him below forty kilometers per hour
most of the time. It took us almost an hour and a half to go
what I estimated to be thirty kilometers. The Italian slowed
the Volks down to a crawl and we crept through a village
that was a cluster of stone houses and what looked to be a
combination café and general store.

"From here we take the horses," he said.

"Where's here?" I asked.

"It's called Trnovo," he said, "and it's not much."

Just past the village we stopped at a small stone house that had a long low shed attached to it.

"Wait here," he said and got out.

He knocked on the door of the house and I caught a glimpse of a tall dark man with a mustache that drooped solemnly down the sides of his heavy chin. Then the Italian was inside the house and the door closed.

"What is he doing?" Tavro said.

"I don't know," I said. "Asking directions maybe."

"He said something about horses," Tavro said.

"That's right."

"When's the last time you were on a horse, Phil?" Wisdom said.

I thought a moment. "Nineteen forty-two, in Columbus, Ohio. It wasn't really a horse though; it was a Shetland pony and it cost a nickel to ride around the ring. I was six or seven, I think."

"I've never been on a horse," Arrie said.

"Maybe you'll like it," I said.

Tavro was sputtering. "It is—it is ridiculous. It is play-acting."

"It's the only transportation there is," I said. "I don't think we'll have to go far."

"The last time I was on a horse," Knight said, "was when I rode into Dodge City ten years ago looking for some mean son of a bitch who'd killed my pard."

"What were you gonna do if you found him, Rafe?" Wisdom said.

"As I recollect, I was gonna shoot him down like a yella dog."

"The marshal stop you?"

"No, as a matter of fact, the mean son of a bitch got me first, but then the marshal got him."

"Maybe I knew your pard," Wisdom said. "How'd he call himself?"

"Went by the name of Carstairs," Knight said. "Jimmy Carstairs."

The Italian came out of the house and opened the door to the Volks. "Around in back," he said.

The snow was almost a foot deep on the path that led to the long low shed and it spilled over into my shoes. My feet were thoroughly wet by the time we entered the shed. I looked around and none of the others wore boots except for the Italian.

The shed was illuminated by a lone kerosene lamp which was held by the man with the mustache. He hung the lamp on a nail and then busied himself with five small horses that were stabled on the right side of the shed. On the left side was a new tan Porsche. The Italian came over to me and held something out.

"Here're the keys to Killingsworth's car," he said as I took them. "I expect he wants it back."

"What about that guy?" I said, nodding toward the man with the mustache.

"He won't be here," the Italian said. "He's with us."

"Who owns this place?" I said.

The Italian looked at me sourly. "When you gonna ask me for my home address?"

"Sorry," I said. "I was just thinking of the cops."

"Let me worry about them."

"Okay," I said. "I will. How far is it?"

"To the castle?"

"Yes."

"Five kilometers. Straight up almost."

"It sounds like a tough ride."

He gave me another sour look. "At least you'll ride," he said. "I've got to walk." He turned and looked at the man with the mustache who nodded and slapped one of the horses on the rump. "Okay," the Italian said. "Get on the horses. Get on from the left side. If you need any help, let me know."

Arrie needed help, so did Gordana. I probably did but I was too proud to admit it. The horses were small animals, ponies really, I think, with shaggy coats that smelled of pine trees and manure. The saddles were wooden affairs with splits down their centers. The Italian and the man with the mustache came down the line checking stirrups.

"You know how to ride?" the Italian asked me.

"No."

He sighed and took my horse by the bridle and led it around the one that Wisdom sat. "Up here with the rest of the girls," he said to me. "Hold the reins in your left hand. You can hold on to the saddle with your right. Don't try to tell the horse what to do, just let him follow."

I turned to look around. Knight was last, sitting his horse casually, as if he knew what he was doing. Wisdom was in front of him. He'd probably learned to ride at school, but I didn't ask. Tavro was behind me and it was evident that he knew how to ride. Gordana was in front of me and Arrie was in front of her.

The Italian looked back at us. He shook his head wearily and then started to speak in that high strained voice that people use who're not accustomed to speaking to groups of more than three.

"We're gonna follow a path for about five kilometers. Try to stay together. If you fall off, try to fall off on the right side. Don't try nothing fancy. Just stay on your horse. When they go up, lean forward. It's gonna take about an hour."

He turned and grasped the bridle of Arrie's horse and we moved out of the shed. The man with the lantern closed the doors behind us. The horses picked their way through the snow which got steadily deeper. Nobody spoke and the only sounds were those of the horses when they snorted and the creaking of the wooden saddles and the leather stirrups.

Ahead of us the Italian used a flashlight to pick his way through the trees. Sometimes its beam illuminated large gray boulders. The path, if that's what it was, led steeply upwards and the horses snorted and shuddered and blew their frosty breath into the icy air. I wondered how cold it was. I knew it was well below freezing and my wet feet were growing numb. I wore gloves and the tweed topcoat, but except for that, I was dressed to spend an evening in some cozy bar, not on top of an animal who moved as if his feet had piles.

The path narrowed and occasionally the branch of a pine, a fir, or some other coniferous brand would belt me across the face, leaving a bitter taste of resined snow. Ahead of me I could make out the dim outline of Gordana as she jogged and weaved in her saddle.

The path or trail became even steeper in grade and I had to lean forward as my pony took small, jarring jumps to get from one level to the next. He seemed to know what he was doing so I held on to the saddle and let him do it. My right coat sleeve occasionally brushed against an outcropping of rock. I poked my left hand out, but it felt nothing. Just space.

Ahead the flashlight beam bobbed and jittered in the blackness.

I was straining to keep my eyes on Gordana's outline when her horse stumbled and she fell from the saddle with a long shrill scream. I slid off my horse into almost two feet of snow and floundered toward the sound. I could see almost nothing. My left foot slipped and I felt myself falling before an arm grabbed me around the neck and pulled me back over the sharp edge of some rock that dug into my back. It was the Italian. He flashed his light into my face and said, "Was that you that screamed?"

"The girl," I said.

He aimed his flashlight down and I could see that we were on a narrow ledge, not more than seven feet wide that cropped out from the side of almost vertical rock cliff.

"If she went over, she's gone," the Italian said in a no-nonsense tone.

He flashed his light down over the edge of the trail and nine feet below us we saw Gordana crouched on a narrow ledge, clinging to the side of the rock with hands that seemed able to find something to hold to when there was nothing in sight. Her face was turned up toward us, her mouth a black, round O of despair.

"Don't move, kid," the Italian said to her softly. "Call the big guy, the good-looking one," he said to me. I yelled for Knight.

"She's not bad, is she?" the Italian said. "In fact, she's a beauty." He could have been commenting on a dozen daisies.

Knight knelt down beside us. "See her down there?" the Italian said, shining his light on Gordana.

"Uh," Knight said.

"Well, you take a leg and I take a leg and we lower St.

Ives down so that he can grab her and then we pull them both back up. How's that?"

"Succinct," Knight said. "You ready?" he asked me.

"Did I ever tell you about me and heights?" I said. "I don't function well."

"You got a better idea?" the Italian said.

"None."

"Get the other American," the Italian said. I yelled for Wisdom this time and when he got there the Italian handed him the flashlight. "Keep it right on her," he said. Wisdom lay on his belly in the snow and shined the light on Gordana whose mouth was now opening and closing silently as if she were gasping great gulps of air.

The Italian took my right leg and Knight took my left one. I felt myself being lowered over the side. I didn't see anything because I had my eyes closed. I didn't open them until I heard someone yelling my name.

"Goddamn it, St. Ives, grab her hands!" Wisdom yelled.

I looked down. Gordana had released her hold on the side of her cliff and was stretching her hands up to me. I tried for them and our fingers brushed, but we missed.

"Please," she cried, "please."

I tried again, stretching as far as I could, but again our fingertips just brushed and this time she lost what balance she had and started to fall and then she screamed and somehow I lunged and caught her left wrist with my right hand. I held on until I got my left hand around her wrist. I had her then, but I knew it wouldn't last long because her wrist was wet and it was beginning to slip through my hands.

"Pull, damn you," I yelled and I began to feel them lifting us slowly, but not fast enough because all I now had was her hand and it was beginning to go. "Faster," I screamed and they tried and her nails dug into my palms as she fought against dying.

There wasn't anything I could do. I looked into her face which was full of mute pleading that begged me not to let her go, but all I had were her fingers now and they began to slip away. And then someone landed on my back, his legs locked around my waist. It was the Italian and he grabbed Gordana's wrist just as her fingers slipped from my grasp. Using his legs to climb with, he worked his way up over my hips dragging Gordana after him. I could hear Knight and Wisdom swear as they pulled on my legs which now supported both Gordana and the Italian. Then I was hanging only by one leg as someone grabbed the Italian and pulled him up. I closed my eyes again.

"Who's got me?" I called.

"I have, I think," Wisdom said.

"Could you sort of pull me up, if it's not too much bother?"

"Wait a second."

"Stick your other leg up," Knight said.

"I thought it was," I said and felt hands on my right ankle. They began to pull.

"How's the view?" Wisdom said.

"Vertiginous," I said, proud that I could think of the word, and then I was over the edge and lying in the snow next to Gordana. Her face was turned toward me and she was crying.

"Thank you, Philip," she said softly. "Thank you so much."

"I almost dropped you," I said.

"You were very brave."

I smiled a little and tried to remember if anyone had ever told me that before.

CHAPTER **25**

We had stopped. My pony jerked his head and snorted again. The flashlight bobbed its way back toward me and the Italian caught the bridle of my pony.

"This is it," he said.

"What?"

"You walk from here."

I slid down from the horse into a couple of feet of snow. My feet were numb.

"I don't see a hell of a lot," I said.

The Italian shined his flashlight ahead and it revealed a large gray boulder. "You go around that rock and up about fifty feet and you're there."

"The castle?"

He sighed as if he were sick of the whole mess. I was ready to agree with him. "It's not a castle. It's just part of what's left of a castle, one of the main halls. They turned it into a kind of a hunting lodge and there're a lot of rooms upstairs

227

that they taught the kids in when it was a school. We just used the main hall."

"Where's Killingsworth?" I said.

"By the fire."

"Just sitting there?"

"You can untie him."

"What about the horses?"

"What about them?"

"I was wondering how we'd get back."

The Italian shined his light in my face. Then he flicked it off. I was blinded—or might as well have been. "How you get back is your problem," he said. "My problem is making sure that you don't get back too soon. The horses go with us." He said something then in Serbo-Croatian and he got a guttural answer from a voice I hadn't heard before.

"This is my partner," the Italian said. "You don't have to see what he looks like, do you?"

"I'll just imagine something," I said.

"Okay. You get the women off and I'll get the rest of them."

I waded through the snow to Gordana's pony. "We walk from here," I said and reached up and helped her down. She seemed weak. "Just stand here by your horse."

Arrie was already down from hers. "What's going on?" she said.

"We walk the rest of the way," I said. "It's not far."

"Who was the man who came by?" she said.

"The Italian's partner," I said. "Did you get a good look at him?"

"No," she said. "Should I've?"

"It doesn't matter."

I could hear the rest of them talking as they dismounted. Then the Italian came up to us and took the reins of Arrie's horse. He handed me the flashlight. "We got another one," he said.

I started to shine the flashlight around but he forced it down. "You don't really wanta get a look at him, do you?" the Italian said.

"I don't give a damn about him. I just want to see if you've collected them all."

"They're right behind me," he said.

I raised my voice. "All right. We have to walk about fifty feet. I'll go first. Then the women. Knight, you come last. Okay?"

"Fine," Knight said. "I'm freezing."

"Everybody is," I said.

"There're some tins of stuff to eat up there and there should be enough wood to last you till morning," the Italian said.

"When we walk back," I said.

"I need the edge," he said. "You object?"

"Would it do any good?"

"No."

"Then I don't object."

I shined the light in the Italian's face. He slapped his hand over his eyes. "Christ," he said.

"Wait here until I take a look around that boulder," I said. "I just want to make sure that there's really something up there."

I waded through the snow and went around the boulder. The beam of the flashlight didn't carry far, but the trail widened through the trees and up ahead there was a large dark mass of something. It could have been a castle or a silent herd of elephants. I turned and made my way back.

"There's something up there," I said.

"It's what I said it was," the Italian said, his voice edged with exasperation. "You just go around that boulder and on about fifty feet and there's a big wooden door. It's not locked. You go through that and you're home. Okay?"

"Okay," I said.

"Okay," he said and led the two horses around me down the trail. He didn't bother to say good-bye.

"Let's go," I said.

We rounded the boulder and waded through the snow for fifty feet until we came to a wall built of wide blocks of gray stone. I shined the flashlight over it and the wall curved slightly. I shined it up and the wall seemed to go up forever. The wooden door that the Italian had promised was there and it was large enough to drive a school bus through. I tugged at the door, but nothing happened. I pushed and it opened easily. I went through followed by Arrie and Gordana, then Wisdom, Tavro, and Knight.

The flashlight revealed an immense bare room with no windows. The walls were coated with a thick gray plaster that looked as if it had been slapped on by hand and smoothed with a stiff brush. A flight of stone stairs with no railing curved up. A dim flickering light came from the top of the stairs. I started up them.

"Look at St. Ives," Wisdom whispered hoarsely, "not a nerve in his body."

"You could follow a man like that through hell itself," Knight said in a deep, reverent voice that almost had me wishing that he wasn't such a good actor.

At the top of the stairs was another large wooden door built of thick planks that was half open. I pushed it all the way open. Across from me, not more than forty feet or so, was a fireplace—the kind that you could walk into and give the steer a couple of turns if it needed it. It made the five-foot logs that burned in it look like a campfire. I glanced up and the ceiling was there all right, not more than twenty-five feet away. The floor was made of slate slabs. I guessed the room itself to be almost sixty feet long and to my right was another stone staircase without railings that ran up the wall and ended at a landing. To my left were tall narrow windows that reached almost from floor to ceiling. They were leaded, but some of the panes were broken. In front of the fireplace was a rough wooden table with benches on either side. Next to the table was an ordinary straight-backed wooden chair. A man sat in it with his hands tied to its arms. He stared at me and I stared back at Amfred Killingsworth, United States Ambassador Extraordinary and Plenipotentiary to the Socialist Federal Republic of Yugoslavia.

I nodded at Killingsworth who only continued to stare at me as I turned and called down the stairs. "Come on up, there's nobody here but the ambassador." It wasn't a bad line.

I walked across the room. "Hello, Killingsworth," I said.

His mouth worked a little before the words came out. I was sure that there would be plenty of them. "You're Phil . . . Phil St.–uh–"

"Ives," I said. "St. Ives."

"You used to work for me."

"Until you fired me."

"Did I?" he said.

"In Chicago."

"I remember now."

I examined the ropes that bound him to the chair. "I'll get you out of these as soon as I get something to cut them with. They been treating you all right?"

"It's been a terrible ordeal," he said and I knew that he was feeling fine.

"Rough, huh?"

Before he could answer the rest of them trooped into the room and headed for the fireplace with only a glance at Killingsworth. If his eyes had popped when they saw me, they bulged at the sight of Tavro and Gordana. Tavro nodded vaguely at Killingsworth as he warmed his hands before the fire. Gordana tried to smile at him but she seemed too worn and cold. I moved over to Arrie.

"Have you got that safety razor?" I said. She nodded and fished around in her large bag with numb hands. She held it out to me. I removed the blade, went back to Killingsworth, and sliced through the ropes that bound his arms and feet. He massaged his hands and then said, "I don't understand. I don't understand what all these people are doing here—what you're doing here. Where're those two men—those two that kidnapped me? They did kidnap me, didn't they? This hasn't been somebody's idea of a wretched joke?"

"No joke," I said. "I'll tell you about it after I get warmed up."

Killingsworth rose and said in a stern voice, "I think you'd better tell me about it now, St. Ives."

"Fuck off, Killingsworth," I said, "I'll tell you about it when I'm goddamned good and ready."

I turned my back on him and walked over to the fire. They were all crowded around it, their hands and feet extended to the blaze. Arrie and Gordana had their shoes off. I looked around for something and finally found a large iron pot. I picked it up and walked across the room, down the stairs, and through the door that led outside. I dipped up a large pot of snow and took it back upstairs.

"Here," I said to the two women, "rub your feet with this. You could have frostbite."

232

"Well, by God, if any man alive could get us through it," Wisdom said, "I knew St. Ives could."

"What's your name, young man?" Killingsworth said, putting his hand on Wisdom's shoulder.

Wisdom popped to attention in his bare feet. "Wisdom, sir. I'm one of the St. Ives Irregulars. He brought us through hell, sir."

"Jesus," I said and tugged off my soaked shoes.

"At the pass, Mr. Ambassador," Knight said in a rich voice full of respect and wonder. "Well, back at the pass I thought for a moment that we were all done for. If it hadn't been for Colonel St. Ives, sir, well, you could have written *finis* to this expedition."

"What are they talking about?" Tavro asked me in a hoarse whisper.

"They're full of frozen shit," I said. "Some of it's just beginning to thaw."

"What're you doing here, Tavro?" Killingsworth said, his big voice booming the question out.

Tavro looked at me and I took a handful of snow and rubbed it on my bare feet. "He's with me, Killingsworth," I said. I looked up at him. He hadn't changed much in thirteen years. His hair was gray now and he wore it the way he always had, so that a thick lock of it fell down across his forehead. He was still handsome except for his blue eyes that were just a little pale and maybe just a little stupid, but then I was prejudiced. It was a big, wide face with a lot of chin and right now the big face looked puzzled and uncertain and I decided it was time to set him straight.

"Near Sarajevo," he said. "They forced my car off the road. It was a new car."

"Then what?"

"They brought me here and made me chop wood. There were two of them, an Italian and another one, a Croat, I think. They threatened to kill me."

"Didn't they tell you anything?"

"They told me I was being held for ransom, but they wouldn't tell me how much or how long I'd have to wait. They didn't tell me anything. I kept asking about my car, but they wouldn't even tell me about that."

"Your car's okay," I said. "The ransom was a million dollars. The government paid it. The kidnappers also demanded the release of Anton Pernik from house arrest and his safe conduct to the border. Gordana was to have gone with Pernik but he died. Tavro took his place. The kidnappers didn't seem to care who came along. Anyway, I was tapped by the State Department to act as go-between in the deal. Mr. Wisdom and Mr. Knight came along to help out. You know Miss Tonzi here. She works for the CIA. I'm not sure why she's along."

"You don't make any sense, St. Ives," Killingsworth said.

"You're not tied to a chair anymore, are you?"

"No."

"Be grateful." I turned back to the fireplace. "Anybody bring any booze?" I said.

"It just so happens that I have a pint of fair bourbon," Wisdom said, handing it over to me.

"You're a treasure, you are," I said and took a long gulp.

"What now?" Arrie said.

"Now?"

"Yes."

I looked at my watch. It was nearly three o'clock. "I'm not planning on walking down any mountain tonight, are you?"

"No."

234

"Then we'll just sprawl around the fireplace and sing songs till it gets light."

"And then?"

I shrugged. "Then you, Killingsworth, Wisdom and Knight can start back for Sarajevo."

"What about Tavro?"

"He and Gordana go with me."

"Where?" she asked.

I grinned at her. "I still don't know."

I looked up and saw that Killingsworth was now talking to Gordana, his big face worked up into an expression of sadness. She was nodding, as if only half listening to what he had to say. Then she shook her head sharply and moved away. Killingsworth looked around as if bewildered, but then I remembered that he'd often looked that way. He saw me and came over to where I sat.

"I have to talk to you privately," he said. "It's important."

I sighed and rose. We went over to the rough wooden table. Killingsworth sat down and hunched over it in what he may have hoped was a conspiratorial manner. "This man Tavro," he said.

"What about him?"

"He's dangerous."

"So."

"He approached me with information. He wanted me to help him get out of the country."

"Did you?"

"No."

"But you took the information."

Killingsworth looked around. "You have no idea how vital it is, St. Ives."

"Hot stuff, huh?"

"It could well determine the future leaders of this country."

"What've you done with it?" I said.

"That's confidential, of course."

"But it's the real thing?"

"There's no doubt about it," he said.

"What do you want me to do?"

"Can you get him out of the country?"

"Maybe."

"I can't be involved, of course."

"Of course."

"But I did more or less promise him."

"In exchange for the information?" I said.

"That's right."

"Well, I can try," I said and started to rise. He used his right hand to pull me back down. "There's one other thing."

"What?"

"I've had a lot of time to think during the past week."

"Uh-huh."

"We've known each other for a long time."

"A half hour ago you couldn't remember my name."

"A man sometimes does foolish things."

"Such as?"

"This girl, Gordana Panić. We were, well, close and I made some promises, some foolish ones, I'm afraid, but now that I've had a chance to think it all through it would be far better if this entire affair didn't involve her. Am I making myself clear?"

"Perfectly," I said. "You want to give her the brush."

Killingsworth frowned. "There's my family to think of."

"What about her?"

236

He ignored the question. "And as ambassador I should avoid any hint of scandal that could damage our relations with Belgrade."

"You want me to fix things, right?"

"Could you?"

"Why should I?"

Maybe I wanted him to crawl a little. Or maybe it was because I thought I'd owed him something for thirteen years and now was my chance to pay it all back with compound interest. His face fell. Crumpled would be better. He was no longer Ambassador Amfred Killingsworth, millionaire publisher. He was only a fifty-year-old man who'd just about wrecked things because of a twenty-two-year-old girl and now he was trying to scramble back, trying to salvage it all, trying to make it as it had been before he fell in love too late in life. And that was probably what hurt most of all, that he couldn't fall in love at fifty with someone who was twenty-two because he didn't have the stomach for the sacrifices that it called for.

"Oh, hell, Killingsworth, I'll see what I can do."

His face brightened. It not only brightened, it shone. "You mean it?"

"Yes."

"I'll remember it, Phil. We've had a few differences, but that's all water under the bridge. Wait till you see my report on how you've handled this. I'll see that you get full credit." He was babbling now, not saying anything really and I only half listened. Then he said, "Who brought you in?"

"Hamilton Coors," I said. "You know him?"

"Of course I know him. Damned fine man. He's a personal friend of mine, the best I've got in the department."

I nodded. It was all that I felt like doing. "Coors speaks well of you, too," I said.

I was dozing by the fireplace about an hour later when I got my first night visitor. It was Tavro. I glanced about and the rest of them were sprawled out or huddled up near the warmth of the flames.

"I must speak with you," Tavro said in his whispering rasp.

"Go ahead."

He looked around, his sad fish face covered with a black and white stubble that made him look mean all the way through. "When will Killingsworth get back to Belgrade?"

"Tomorrow, I think."

"He has information, papers, documents that are mine."

"I thought you gave them to him."

Tavro frowned. "It was a foolish mistake. I must have them back."

"I don't think there's much chance."

"Then I must leave immediately." He started to rise. I caught his arm and pulled him back down.

"You don't have a chance," I said. "We'll try it tomorrow with the girl. You can be her grandfather."

He shook his head. "Mr. St. Ives, if the information that is contained in those documents that I gave your ambassador is revealed to anyone else, I will be dead before night." I looked at him. His face was still grumpy and mean, but it was also serious.

"I don't understand," I said.

"Your ambassador, Mr. Killingsworth, does not have the background to assess their true significance."

"He told me that it was hot stuff."

"He was speaking as a newspaperman, not as a diplomat.

The information that he possesses could destroy this government."

"Isn't that what you want?"

Tavro looked away and then returned his gaze to me. It contained as much sincerity as he was capable of displaying, perhaps more. "Not if it would take Russian tanks, Mr. St. Ives."

"Like Czechoslovakia, huh?"

"You do not believe me?"

"No."

Tavro shook his head and then smiled as if he felt sorry for my stupidity—which he may have. "Think about this, Mr. St. Ives. If I were not telling the truth, I certainly would not be here."

I nodded as he rose. "Okay," I said. "We'll go first tomorrow. The others can come out later."

"Tomorrow," he said, as if he were not at all sure that there would be such a thing. Then he rose and walked to the far end of the fireplace where he stood and looked into the flames for a long time. I watched him for a while and then I tried to go to sleep, and almost succeeded until something warm and wet started licking my ear.

"What're you doing?" It was Arrie, of course.

"Trying to sleep," I said. "Doesn't the sandman stop by your place anymore?"

"I was cold."

I put my arm around her. She snuggled against my chest. "I bet they have rooms upstairs," she said.

"We'd freeze before we got there."

"What did Tavro want?"

"Out."

"You still going to help him?"

"I'm thinking about it."

"You're making a mistake."

"Probably."

"None of it's gone right, has it?"

I looked down at her, but she had turned her face away from me. "None of what?" I said.

"None of what you thought you were supposed to do."

"No, it's all gone wrong."

"It could get worse," she said.

"I don't see how."

She sighed and snuggled closer. "You will if you try to get him out."

CHAPTER **26**

The cold awakened me. Thin gray light was coming through the tall windows. The fire had died down. I gently lifted Arrie's head from my chest and made her a pillow of my topcoat. She curled into it without waking. I rose and went over to the fireplace, put three large logs on, and waited until they caught. I squatted down and warmed my hands before the flames. And then I thought for a long time, until the thinking threatened to become the end itself rather than the method by which the end is reached.

I rose and walked over to the windows. Before me stretched a broad, snow-covered meadow that was lined by thick forests of fir and pine. Beyond the meadow was more forest that rose until it thinned out into snow and rocks and became the peak of a mountain whose name I would like to have known.

Below the castle near the edge of the forest, two deer, a buck and a doe, took small, delicate, tentative steps into the deep snow. They stopped, looked around suspiciously, and then bounded across the meadow, hurrying into the safety of the forest on the other side.

I turned from the window and went back to the fireplace. Tavro was propped up against the stone wall, his overcoat drawn up to his chin. I bent down and shook his arm. He opened his eyes and then opened and closed his mouth several times as if he tasted something bad.

"It's time we started," I said and moved over to where Gordana sat sleeping with her head on Wisdom's shoulder. I shook her gently and she stirred, but didn't open her eyes, and I had to shake her again. She opened her eyes slowly and smiled at me. It was a child's smile that contained a child's faith and I didn't feel that I deserved it.

"It's time," I said and she nodded and stretched. Wisdom also awakened.

"What time is it?" he said.

I looked at my watch. "Nearly seven thirty."

The rest of them began to stir. Killingsworth rose and stretched and looked around as if he felt he should say something, something wise perhaps, like telling the rest of us where the toilet was. He didn't. Knight was up looking rumpled but ruggedly handsome. I envied him. Arrie was the last to awaken. She got up quickly, clutching her purse to her as though she thought someone might snatch it away.

"I think I found some coffee," Wisdom said, poking around in a box of canned goods.

"Make some in that pot that I used for snow," I said. "There should be enough water left in it."

He nodded, opened the paper sack of coffee, and threw a couple of handfuls of the grounds into the pot and hung it over the fire with a metal hook that swung from the wall. I don't think Wisdom did much cooking for himself.

One by one they trooped downstairs and out into the snow to relieve themselves and when they came back they dipped tin cups into the coffee and drank it gratefully even though it was indescribably bad. They turned toward me instinctively, it seemed, even Killingsworth, as though waiting for me to tell them what to do next now that they'd gone to the toilet. I took another sip of the coffee and lit a cigarette.

"I'm going to borrow your car, Killingsworth," I said.

"What's that?"

"I'm going to borrow your car. I need it. Tavro and Gordana are going with me. I want you to give us an hour's start. When you get down to the village Arrie can tell someone who you are and they'll call the authorities. I don't care what you tell them about me."

We were all standing. Tavro, with his coat on, was slightly behind Wisdom. I was next to Gordana, and Knight and Killingsworth were near the fireplace. Arrie was by herself near the table.

"All right," I said, looking at Gordana. "Let's go."

"Tavro's not going." It was Arrie's voice. I turned to look at her. She held a small automatic in her right hand. It was aimed at Tavro. "He's not going any place, Phil. I'm sorry."

"Aw, come on," I said and started toward her. She kept her eyes an Tavro. He looked at me and then at the pistol. His face started working, as if he were trying to think of something to say. Instead, he shoved Wisdom violently at Arrie. The gun went off. Tavro ran toward the open door and through it and I could hear his leather heels clatter down the stairs.

Wisdom stumbled against the table, tried to catch it, but

failed, and fell to the floor on his back. There was a small black and red hole under the pocket of his white shirt. Arrie stood frozen, the gun in her hand, staring at Wisdom, her mouth silently forming the word "No" over and over.

I ran to the window and forced it open. Tavro was in the meadow, trying to run through the deep snow. He floundered, fell, picked himself up, and tried to run again. I yelled at him. "Don't try it, Tavro!"

He may have heard me because he stopped, looked back, and then tried to run again. They cut him down before he got three steps. It sounded like a submachine gun.

I turned from the window and ran back to Arrie who stood motionless, staring down at the fallen Wisdom, the gun still in her hand. I took the gun, ran back to the window, and tossed it into a snow bank. Then I went back to Wisdom. Knight had ripped open Wisdom's shirt and was trying to stop the blood with his handkerchief. I handed him mine as I knelt down beside them.

Wisdom's breath came in harsh wheezes. His eyes were closed. He opened them and looked at Knight. He smiled and shook his head slightly. He turned his eyes and found mine. Once more he shook his head, but only a little. "Don't blame the kid, Phil."

"No," I said, "I don't."

Arrie was kneeling by him now. She was weeping.

"Not your fault, kid," Wisdom said and tried to smile at her and almost made it before the pain hit. He shuddered and closed his eyes tightly and then looked up once more at Knight. This time he did smile, broadly. "Goddamn it, Carstairs," he said, "get back to your post." Then he died.

Knight kept the handkerchiefs pressed to the dead man's chest, even when the metallic words boomed out from the bullhorn. "What's it say?" I asked Arrie, but she was sobbing now. I turned to Gordana who stood, staring blankly down at the dead Wisdom. "The loud-speaker," I said, "what's it saying?"

She didn't look at me. She kept on staring at Wisdom. "It is saying," she said, "that we should come outside with our hands above our heads. It is saying it over and over."

"Listen," I said. "Tavro's been killed. He was shot. Do you all understand?" I looked around. Killingsworth nodded dully. So did Gordana. "You understand, Arrie?" I said. This time she nodded.

"It was a submachine gun," I said. "The same burst that killed Tavro also killed Wisdom. Is that understood?"

Knight raised his head and stared at me. There were tears streaming down his cheeks. They were not the tears of an actor.

"What the fuck are you doing, St. Ives?" he said. "Park's hardly dead, the crap's not even cold in his pants yet, and you're already hustling one of your phony deals. He was a friend of yours, wasn't he? Can't you even let the poor bastard die right? There's something wrong with you, St. Ives. You need something fixed. Now get away from us, goddamnit! Just get the fuck away!"

I moved back and watched Knight as he knelt by Wisdom, his head bent, his shoulders shaking now as he sobbed unashamedly. Arrie touched my arm. I turned and she shook her head slightly. "Don't say it," she said softly. "Don't try to say anything. Not now. Later."

I turned and took her arm and motioned to Killingsworth and Gordana. The four of us went down the stairs and out into the snow with our hands above our heads. Down in the meadow where Tavro had fallen I could see a group of men clad in gray uniforms. There were two other men with them dressed in civilian clothes. One of the civilians turned and pointed at us. The men in uniforms started moving across the meadow in our direction. Other men in uniforms came out of the forest and took up places around the body of Tavro.

The men in uniforms reached us first. They looked at us curiously, their submachine guns aimed in our general direction. When Arrie asked a question, one of them nodded a little shamefacedly.

"He says we can take our hands down," she said.

I watched the two men in civilian clothes come closer. They were both short and they had a hard time making it through the deep snow. The nearest one saw me and waved cheerfully, as if I were liege of the manor and he an invited guest. I didn't wave back at Slobodan Bartak of the Ministry of Interior. I had been expecting him. The man behind Bartak didn't wave at me. He gave me a stony look instead.

It was all I should have expected from Hamilton Coors and the U.S. Department of State.

CHAPTER **27**

They headed for Killingsworth first, of course. He was after all the ambassador and there was protocol to be considered, even at a kidnapping.

I don't know what lies Killingsworth told them. I didn't try to listen. Instead I looked out across the meadow at the mountain peak whose name I would like to have known. Finally, I turned and said to anyone who cared to listen, "I'm going inside. I'm cold."

Bartak turned from Killingsworth. He wore a broad, pleased smile on his face. "Well, Mr. St. Ives, it worked out much as I hoped it would."

"Sure," I said.

"The ambassador is safe and the kidnapper has been apprehended."

"Tavro?" I said.

"Did you suspect that he was the one who engineered the kidnapping?"

I looked at Hamilton Coors. He stared back at me, not blinking, probably not even giving a damn. "No," I said, "I didn't suspect that."

Bartak looked even more pleased, and the glint of early promotion was in his eyes. "Tavro had accomplices, of course. We'll round them up soon enough."

"An Italian," I said, stubbornly keeping my end of the bargain. "One of them was an Italian, about thirty-five. I didn't get a good look at the other one, but I think he was a Croat."

Bartak nodded again, nothing but good humor. "You led us quite a chase," he said.

I nodded. A blind man might have had some difficulty in following the trail I'd blazed across a good section of Yugoslavia. A four-year-old child would have had no trouble at all. The only thing I hadn't done was to drop bread crumbs in the snow.

"It's the way I had to operate," I said and looked again at Hamitlon Coors who returned my gaze, a slight smile on his face now. It could have meant anything or nothing at all.

"I was wondering if you heard the news of your death?" Bartak said, even chuckling a little.

"I heard it."

"Yes, it was simply a matter of wrong identification. The person at your embassy, a Mr. Lehmann, identified the body as being yours, but then he said that you two had only met casually. I must say that the dead man did bear you a striking resemblance."

"Who was he?" I said.

"We're not yet sure," Bartak said, "but we suspect that he somehow may have been involved in the kidnapping."

"Because of where he was found?" I said.

Bartak dropped a little of his early morning good humor. "Yes, because of where he was found, almost directly across the street from Tavro's house. A cottage really. He grew roses."

"So he told me," I said.

Hamilton Coors eased into the conversation, smooth as greased marble. "I really should talk to Mr. St. Ives about several matters, Mr. Bartak," he said, taking my arm and steering me toward the castle before I blew the whole thing.

"There's a dead man upstairs," I said. "A friend of mine."

"Really?" Hamilton Coors said. "We'll have to do something about that, won't we?"

Coors stood at the window of one of the small, bare upstairs rooms and looked out over the meadow. He rocked easily up and down on his toes, his hands clasped behind his back which was turned toward me.

"You didn't want me to get him out, did you?" I said.

"Tavro?"

"Who else?"

"Your question's hardly germane," he said, "since you never had the slightest intention of trying to." He turned around. "However, it worked out most satisfactorily, don't you think?"

"What was Tavro's real pitch?"

"Oh, he had information all right."

"Was it any good?"

"Why do you ask?"

"He parted with it too easily. He handed it over to Killingsworth and then asked for help. After he handed it over it didn't leave him any leverage. That's why I say that he seemed more interested in peddling his information than he was in leaving the country."

Coors turned away from me and walked over to a wall. He inspected it to see whether it was clean enough to lean against. It was and he leaned against it, his arms folded across his chest. He had on a suit different from the one that I'd seen him in last, a dark green one with pale gray stripes. The search that he had made for a tie had been worth it.

"What did he tell you about his information?" he said.

"That it could bring Russian tanks into Belgrade. Could it?"

Coors frowned and walked back to the window and let me look at his back again. "The CIA thinks so."

"And you don't?"

"I didn't say that."

"But Tavro wanted the information broadcast."

"Tavro and the people behind him. They wanted somebody else to do it, of course. Preferably the Americans." Coors turned around again. "Why did you go through with it?"

I shrugged. "I don't know."

"You must have known that the CIA was mixing in. You must have known that early on."

"It was. They tried to bribe me."

"How much?"

"Ten thousand pounds."

Coors shook his head. "They like to spend money. It does something for them."

"They first approached me in New York, but I didn't know it was the CIA then. They even arranged a phony hit-and-run."

"The same chap?"

I nodded. "Your security wasn't too good. He was waiting for me in the lobby of my hotel when I got back. He was playing at being Artur Bjelo then."

Coors tugged at his lower lip. "We saw that it was leaked to them just after you left Washington. We wanted to see how fast they'd move."

"They met me at the airport in Belgrade."

"The Tonzi girl?"

I nodded. "She accidentally shot my friend. Bartak doesn't have to know about it though."

"No," Coors said, "he doesn't. Have you—uh—tried to arrange things?" I nodded and there was a brief silence.

"Who killed Stepinac?" I said.

Coors shrugged. "Tavro's people, I assume. They thought that he was going to tip you off about Tavro."

"You mean that Tavro really didn't want out of the country?"

This time Coors only nodded. "That was all part of his sales pitch, of course—to give his information a dash of authenticity, although it really didn't need it."

"He added another touch when he got an old friend of his killed," I said. "An American."

"I heard about him," Coors said. "Was his name really Bill Jones?"

I nodded. "Jones's house was bugged. He was supposed to set up a meeting between me and Tavro. He wasn't able to get in touch with Tavro, but the meeting came off anyhow. That puzzled Jones a bit before he died. It also puzzled me for a while."

There was a brief silence and then I asked, "What are you going to do with Tavro's information?"

"Sit on it."

"What's the CIA want to do?"

Coors looked up at the ceiling and pursed his lips. "That's really the crux of the matter, I suppose. That's why Tavro died. If Tavro had found out that we weren't going to use the information, he might have peddled it to someone else. The French perhaps. The CIA didn't want that, of course. If they couldn't have it themselves, they didn't want anyone else to have it. It's their dog in the manger attitude really."

"But you've got it," I said. "Or at least Killingsworth does."

"Ah," Coors said. "But they know that we won't use it, so it's just as if we really don't have it. It's quite a subtle point, don't you think?"

"The CIA wouldn't have used it," I said. "They wouldn't have brought tanks into Belgrade."

"Of course not," Coors said. "But they would have bargained with it. They would have gotten something they wanted. That's why they tried to delay the exchange. They wanted time to try to get the information from Tavro. Failing that, they had him killed so nobody else could get it."

I shook my head. "You had him killed really. You set him up."

Coors decided to inspect his fingernails. "We don't operate quite that way."

"You don't have to," I said. "Tavro was trying to give authenticity to his information by lying about how bad he needed to get out of the country. So you obliged him. You turned him over to me. You might as well have killed him."

"If you had tried, you might have succeeded."

"But I had no intention of trying. You knew that. That's the real reason you hired me. You wanted something to happen to Tavro. It did."

"Yes," Coors said. "I suppose it did." He looked around the room. "How did Killingsworth take his ordeal?"

"He's over his romance."

Coors smiled a little. "A passing fancy, I suppose."

252

"I want the girl out," I said.

"The granddaughter?"

I nodded.

He shook his head. "I don't think that can be arranged."

"Find a way," I said. "She'd like to go to New York. You can also find a way to pay for it for a year or two."

"What's she to you?" Coors said.

"Nothing. It's just that she should be something to someone."

He again shook his head.

"Find a way," I said, "or Killingsworth finds out how you've played him for a fool. That's my ace."

"I was wondering what you would want when you played it," Coors said.

"Now you know."

He looked at me curiously. "Don't you grow tired of blackmail?"

"Sure," I said. "I'm sick of it. But it doesn't make me as sick as it did to watch a friend of mine get killed for no good reason that I can think of, unless they're the ones that you've just given me and they're worse than no reasons at all. Watching my friend die made me really sick. So blackmail doesn't bother me much anymore. It doesn't even make me queasy."

"All right," Coors said. "I'll take care of the girl."

"Thanks."

"But don't blame me for your friend's death."

"I'm not blaming you," I said. "I'm blaming the stupidity of your system. It doesn't have to work like that."

Coors began to pace up and down. He paced quite a while before he said anything.

"You can't blame the system," he said slowly, "if that's what you want to call it, because we're all products of the system.

But that doesn't excuse some of the mistakes it makes out of sheer inadvertence or carelessness or—as you say—stupidity. It doesn't excuse them at all."

He paused to look at me carefully. "Still, the system protects us and that's why we have to protect it. If we start tinkering with it, messing around with its insides, then we might change it so radically that it would no longer protect us—couldn't even if it wanted to."

He nodded then, as if making the next point to himself. "We have to change it, of course, from time to time. It's far from perfect. But we mustn't be stampeded into it. Careful, systematic development is the answer, not radical improvisation. Otherwise, we might destroy it, imperfect though it may be, and replace it with something far worse."

When Coors was through he looked quickly around and then chuckled, almost as if he were a bit embarrassed. "Quite a little lecture, wasn't it? Although I'm not at all sure that it did you any good."

"No," I said, "I don't think it did either. Not me anyway. But I know of someone you should try it on."

"Who?"

"A guy called Carstairs," I said. "He really likes crap like that."